THE PERFECT ENDING

A NOVEL

ROB KAUFMAN

<u>Other books by Rob Kaufman</u>

One Last Lie

A Broken Reality

In the Shadow of Stone

ALTERED
(Justin Wright Series – Book 1)

To those I've loved and lost –
You live in my heart, my imagination
and every word I write.

PROLOGUE

Artie Majewski had a bad feeling as soon as he hung up with Central.

In twenty-plus years with Metro-North, this wasn't the first time he'd gotten a five o'clock wakeup to sub on the Harlem Line. No, the creepy feeling was because of what Karen had said when the phone rang. "Bad things come in threes," she'd muttered before drifting off to sleep again. And given the way his luck had been lately, Artie suspected his wife was right.

It all started the night before at Paddy's—seventh-inning versus the Red Sox, Yanks up by three, and Ray O'Malley running his mouth. Artie often bragged to his buddies that he could do his job with his eyes closed, but he should've known better than to bring up the new PTC system they were installing. Trying to explain it to Ray was like trying to explain quantum physics to a squirrel. Artie had to tell him three times that PTC stood for Positive Train Control, and even after he detailed how Central used GPS to track trains and slow them down, the moron had the balls to say, "Now you really *can* do your job with your eyes closed!" Artie was so pissed off, he bet Ray double or nothing on the ballgame—which ended up biting him in the ass when the Yanks lost on a grand slam in the ninth. A hundred bucks down the drain.

Yeah, that was number one—the *first* bad thing to happen.

1

And now here he was, raking his fingers through his thinning hair, trying to breathe the humid air that hung like molasses inside the overheated train cab. His hangover had tapered off to a dull ache behind his eyes, but he could still hear Ray and those other douchebags laughing as if they were sitting right there beside him. This wasn't the first PTC system he'd tested, but he certainly didn't expect to be dicking around with it on his day off, nor did he like that Central kept making him stop the train. This time he was a mile out of Hartsdale. Almost fifteen minutes now he'd been waiting— something about "refreshing the data in the monitoring system." Whatever the hell that meant.

Artie tried again to take a deep breath and fixed his eyes on the heat waves squiggling up from the stretch of empty track before him. Temp gauge on the dash read ninety-one outside, and inside wasn't much better. Artie could feel the sweat trickling down his back and under the folds of his flabby pecs. How many millions Metro-North spent on PTC and they still couldn't get the friggin' air conditioning to work?

Artie glanced up at the camera that monitored his every move and threw up his hands with a silent *"Hurry up!" gesture*. A few seconds later, the signal light on his dash turned from red to green.

"All clear," said the voice on the radio. Artie gave the camera a half-salute with one hand, and with the other, pushed forward on the accelerator stick.

Finally, he was moving again —

The only good thing about today was the new M8 he was driving—like a damn spaceship compared to the old M6 shit-buckets he used to drive. The Hudson Line had had the M8s for years now—and, of course, it had been the first to get the PTC after some new guy fell asleep in the cab and took a thirty-mile-per-hour turn at eighty a few years back. Lots of people dead, a bunch more injured. What a freaking shit show caused by a lazy dipshit.

But today, Artie was the one who felt like a dipshit. He should've been sleeping off his hangover, but no, he had to go and put his name in for overtime, and sure enough, the call at five told him to be at Grand Central by seven. Karen didn't know about the hundred he'd lost to Ray the night before, but she was still right in theory: the phone call was number two – the *second* bad thing that happened.

Artie cursed himself and kicked the train's speed up to seventy. The light on the dash immediately started blinking red, and then the PTC kicked in and the train slowed down to the posted sixty-five.

"All clear," Artie radioed back to Central, and the controller gave him a quick, "*Check.*" The plan from up top had been for him to test out the M8's new system one last time with no passengers, and then they could get the train officially online for the afternoon rush. But now, with all the stops and data refresh crap, Artie wasn't sure they were going to make it. Neither was Central, apparently—which was why they greenlighted him through Hartsdale at thirty-five. It'd be the same for Scarsdale, it looked like, as he approached the station a few minutes later.

And then he saw the guy at the end of the platform.

Maybe it was how he was standing that tipped Artie off—tense, leaning slightly forward with his feet too close to the edge. Or just maybe, it was the bug Karen put in his ear that morning. Either way, Artie somehow knew the *third* bad thing was about to happen.

He'd never had a jumper, but he'd certainly heard the stories of people being pushed or leaping in front of the train out of nowhere. It all happened so fast, the engineers always said, but for Artie Majewski, everything next unfolded slowly—almost as if he were seeing it *before* it happened.

At least, that's how he would explain it to Karen later that night, when the half bottle of Dewar's he'd polished off finally stopped his hands from shaking. In one moment, there was the guy leaning way too far over the edge of the platform, and in the next, there was this young blonde woman wearing a bright red tee-shirt reaching for his arm as if she knew what was about to happen.

Artie shouldn't have been able to see it all in such detail as the PTC kicked in—sixty to fifty to thirty-five. "But it was like I was on a conveyor belt or something," he told Karen. "Like a dream, you know, where you're moving but at the same time you're frozen?" And yet, Artie *wasn't* frozen—at least according to the cab footage, which clearly showed him switching on the PTC's manual override to slow the train down faster.

But still, years later, and long after he'd hung up his engineer's cap for good, Artie Majewski would bolt awake in the middle of the night—his cries of, "Don't do it!" muffled and thick with weeping as the train's brakes screeched back at him from the dark.

4

CHAPTER 1

Scott Atwood stood before the soaring picture windows that overlooked the still, mirror-like creek behind his home. The man-made canal was extremely narrow–small enough for the ducks to paddle from one side to the other, but large enough for Scott to feel completely separated from the homes on the other shore. His eyes fixed on a gaggle of geese silently treading their way through the water and around the boulders. Sipping his coffee, he envied the birds' calm disposition as he tried to come up with the best way to kill himself.

He knew it had to be spectacular – something dramatic that would seize the headlines of every TV station, newspaper and online news outlet. *For Christ's sake, I'm one of the most popular thriller-suspense authors in the world.* He turned to the books that filled his living room bookcase. *Fifteen New York Times bestsellers, five Edgar awards, three National Book Critics Circle Awards. My death must be powerful, everlasting. Nothing mundane like hanging myself or swallowing a bottle of pills.*

And slitting his wrists was a definite no-go. More likely than not, it would be his ex-wife, Sheila, who would find him in the bathtub, soaking in a pool of his own blood, after hunting him down in hopes of getting her AMEX Platinum Card renewed. She'd immediately make herself the main attraction and his name would vanish from the news as quickly as she'd spend her inheritance.

He took another sip of coffee and turned toward his office door at the other side of the living room. With a glance at the phone on his desk, his tension grew. His agent, Grace, would be calling any moment to request an update about his latest novel. He'd been putting off this call for weeks. The only update he had was that there *was* no update.

Since his January 1st resolution to start his next novel, it was as though his creativity went MIA. He'd been unable to drum up a single concept that would take hold and allow him to thread together the pieces of a thrilling puzzle, another suspenseful masterpiece.

For the past eight months, he'd spent countless hours pacing and murmuring to himself the basic elements of writing a story, the five components he'd learned in fifth grade and right now couldn't find to save his life: *setting, characters, plot, conflict, resolution.* Over and over he'd repeat them, stumbling from room to room and floor to floor inside his idyllic, Westchester Colonial. But his imagination never showed up and the fact that he had nothing to give Grace made him realize it was a hopeless endeavor. His insides were hollow, his creativity cleaned out. His career was over. Something had emptied his reservoir of inventive spirit and without it, writing had become impossible. And so had living.

August would be a good month to die, he thought. It didn't rain too much in Westchester, New York this time of year, so the throngs of people who'd want to attend his funeral could do so without worrying about getting wet. Of course, it might be a bit hot for some, but he'd make sure that his suicide note included instructions that all attendees receive a handheld fan to help keep cool. He wanted to be sure any post-funeral remarks would be positive. But he'd take care of all of that later. Right now he had to figure out exactly how he should end his life so that he'd always be remembered by his current fans, and revered by future generations.

His mind wandered to Vincent Van Gogh... Virginia Woolf... Gregory Gillespie. Great artists who had taken their own lives, but in ways that were much too pedestrian for his taste. No, his death had to be...

The phone's ring made him jump and spill coffee onto his favorite Ishfahan rug. He glanced at the splotch, then to the phone, then back to the splotch. He had no doubt he could make the spot disappear, but knew he wouldn't be able to do the same with Grace. She'd keep calling until he answered or, if her patience wore too thin, she'd send the cops over to bang down his door. She wanted the first draft of his new novel and if she had to she'd bring in the FBI to hunt through every drawer or laptop file until they found what she needed.

He raced into his office and grabbed the phone.

"Gracie!" He feigned excitement. "I've been waiting for your call."

Scott placed his coffee cup on a coaster, sat down in his Herman Miller chair, leaned back and crossed his feet on the edge of the desk.

Grace was barking orders at her assistant, her voice as raspy as ever. Actually, she could've been squawking at her boss for all Scott knew, but he didn't ask because she still hadn't responded to his greeting. Maybe he should just hang up.

"Hold on a second, Scotty."

Damn it. The knot in his stomach tightened.

"And don't forget Freddy's check," he heard her yell. "I'm sorry, Scotty. There's so much going on in my life right now, I can't keep things straight. But we'll get to that in a minute. Let me shut the door." He heard her heels clapping on what sounded like a wood floor. That meant she wasn't in her Madison Avenue office, but in her home office in Amsterdam, a location where she could release her full rage and fury without any repercussions.

Shit.

"How are you?" She was slightly out of breath.

"I'm good," he sighed. "I guess I shouldn't ask how *you* are." His feet tapped nervously on the chair mat and he considered making a dash to the minibar to grab a shot of Johnny Walker. He rolled his eyes at himself. By the time the booze kicked in, the call would be over.

I'm screwed.

"No, don't ask about me, because we have to deal with first things first. Please tell me you're a lot further along on your next book than the last time we spoke."

The response Scott had practiced for three days and had considered perfect just yesterday suddenly didn't seem to be enough. Before he had a chance to come up with another respectable retort, Grace was demanding, "You're kidding me, right, Scott? Please tell me you're done with the manuscript or *close* to done. Give me something. Craig is down my throat, up my ass and screwing me sideways. He's fighting with the head of publishing, the printer and even the press. Everyone's waiting for me to tell them something and I have nothing. Not even a blurb... an elevator pitch. I've got nothing! You've given me nothing!"

Scott heard her take three deep breaths. She'd once told him her meditation guru taught her how to do a special type of breathing three times in such a way; it should calm her down immediately. Unfortunately, it never worked. "Scott. God damn it! Talk to me."

The anxiety in her voice made something in his brain click.

An idea? Could this be a real idea forming in my head right now?

Although she was sucking the last sliver of patience he had left after the past eight months of anguish, the thought that a new idea was brewing stopped him from stringing together a line of vulgarities and hanging up on her — especially since it was her intense frustration that sowed the seed of this idea.

"Before I tell *you* about the book, tell me what's going on in your life. You know, all this shit that's making you sound like a nutjob struggling inside a straitjacket."

"Don't, Scott. Don't fill this conversation with my bullshit when it's *your* bullshit that keeps me employed and makes us both a lot of money. I'm not going to..."

Scott knew if there was a true concept germinating in his head, he had to hear more about what was going on in her life. This new book could start right here, right now, with Grace's crazy-ass problems.

"Jesus Christ, Gracie. Just take another one of your breaths, calm down and tell me what's going on. I promise, after that, I'll tell you all about my next book."

Silence.

"Grace?"

"Yes, I heard you. Okay, Scott. If that's what it's going to take to get you to talk, I'll do it." She paused and took another deep breath. "Here's my life in a nutshell. Missy, my eighteen-year-old, decided this week that she's a lesbian. Next week, who knows? This week, she's a lesbian. Jocelyn, my twenty-year-old, is at UCLA living with her father, who is, as of three months ago, cohabitating with a twenty-five-year-old. Her name is Mandy. Jocelyn and Mandy hang out together during the day, go home and then Mandy and Joe screw all night. I can't deal with the thought of... And you remember Frederick, right? He's my twenty-two-year-old you met at the release party I threw for *Don't Be Fooled*. He can't seem to figure out what he wants to do with his life, other than finding ways to destroy my Beemer so it's in the shop every other week. Oh, and I've gone on two dates over the past three months. One of them almost ended with me calling 9-

THE PERFECT ENDING —

1-1 because his hands were boob magnets. Then on the second date I again considered calling 9-1-1 because the guy was so boring I thought I'd need resuscitation." Grace stopped talking and sighed. "Have you heard enough yet?"

Scott felt trembling inside his gut. The spark of an idea had turned into a wildfire.

"Yes, I've heard enough."

"Okay, now tell me. What've you got for me?"

Scott cleared his throat. The words he was about to utter would be as unfamiliar to him as they were going to be to Grace. "So, there's this author... a psychological thriller author who can't think of an idea for his next book."

"Scott, please don't tell me –"

"Hold on, Grace. Just hold on for one Goddamn second." The sliver of patience had completely dissolved.

"Ouch," she muttered.

"I'm sorry. You just have to let me talk."

"I'm listening."

"So this author's life is so boring and lacks such passion and excitement, he can't come up with a character, a plot, a twist, anything that would keep a reader turning the pages. So he decides to wreak havoc in other people's lives in order to come up with ideas for his next book."

He heard her breathing stop and closed his eyes, awaiting a response. As an agent, Grace knew her shit. She had good instincts as to what would sell and what wouldn't. She didn't realize it, but her reaction to his idea could mean the difference between life or death. *His* life or death.

"Hmmmm." She cleared her throat. "Have you started it yet?"

"I'm seventy-five percent done. It's amazing. Better than *Don't Be Fooled* and ten times better than *Dying to Tell.*"

Grace gasped. "*Dying to Tell* was your all-time best seller! This can't be better!"

"Trust me," Scott responded, attempting to assure himself as much as Grace. "It'll beat *Don't Be Fooled* from sales to movie gross once it hits the theaters."

"When do I get to read it? We should probably send the first few chapters to editing so they can start..."

Scott leaned forward and rolled the chair to the center of his desk, directly in front of the laptop. He looked at the screen. It was as blank as it had been eight months ago with the exception of two words: Chapter One.

"Honestly, Grace. This book is different than the others... in ways I can't explain without giving too much away. I really need to wait 'til I'm done before letting anyone see it." *Is she buying this bullshit?* He had to cut her uncertainty off at the pass. "I'll have it to you in one week... two weeks max. I promise."

"Scotty," she moaned. "I have no idea how you've built an entire book around this concept, but I trust you. You're the genius, so I'll leave it in your hands. I can expect the manuscript emailed in seven to fourteen days, right? And not *business days*. Fourteen days, including weekends."

"If not before," Scott said, his shattered nerves still begging for a scotch. "Now let me get back to work."

"Okay, okay. I'll update Craig and the others. And please let me know if there's anything I can do to help get it here sooner."

"Yeah, yeah. Always pushing me for your own benefit," he said jokingly, but meaning every word. "And good luck with your kids, your ex-husband, Mandy, the Beemer and all your future dates. Sounds like you need it."

"I need more than just luck, Scotty. I need a new life. But as Master TigiGama says, 'breeeathe... breeeathe.' So I will do as he says as I wait *patiently* for your manuscript."

"You got it, love. Thanks for your patience."

"Don't thank me yet. Gotta go. Hurry up, please."

Before Scott had a chance to respond, Grace had hung up.

Scott did the same, slamming down his laptop cover and covering his face with his hands.

Can I make this idea work? Is there really something to it?

Grabbing his coffee cup, he walked to the kitchen for a refill. With his first sip, he closed his eyes and the anger swelled in his gut. He'd just screwed himself by adding to his indecision. Five minutes ago, the only choice he had to make was how to kill himself. Now he had to decide *if* he'd kill himself or try to make this idea work.

He walked to the French doors beside the giant windows, slid one open and stepped onto the balcony. The same geese were treading water, the same creek was as still, quiet and as uninteresting as his life. The only sound was the faint echo of a train's horn coming from somewhere in the distance.

That's it! The perfect way to commit suicide hit him like a freight train – which was exactly what he intended to do. Or at least a passenger train which would be much easier to get to. If he threw himself in front of a train, the local news would have it on the wires within minutes. Once they discovered the victim was Scott Atwood, it would be online and shooting across the major news networks within the hour. People would never know if it was deliberate, an accident, or if it might've even been murder. He could make this the perfect ending for an author who consistently gave his fans a thrilling finale to his books – an outcome that always created as much excitement as it did uncertainty.

But what about the idea he'd told Grace? Could he really write a psychological thriller with a plot like that?

Setting, characters, plot, conflict, resolution. Can this story actually have those things? Should it take place in Manhattan? No, everyone does that. Chicago? No, another overdone city. What about the character? Should the protagonist be based on Grace's situation? She'd freak out if her kids made the connection and discovered Grace aired their dirty laundry. What about Sheila? No, she isn't worthy of any recognition, especially in a Scott Atwood thriller. Jesus Christ! Here's that freakin' writer's block again...

"Stop freaking out," he said aloud, gazing into the cloudless sky. "You know what you have to do." Scott knew there was only one way to decide between trying to make his new idea work and taking his own life: he had to have both choices with him at the same time. He made his way back inside the house to his office, grabbed his laptop and slid it under his arm. He then swiped his car keys off his desk, threw on his sunglasses and baseball cap and took one last look at the creek before heading toward the front door. Scarsdale was the closest train station. It was there he'd sit on a platform bench with his laptop and see if there was any substance to his story about a defeated, empty author.

If there was, he'd type non-stop, without effort, like he always did when the juices were flowing. If there wasn't, there would always be another train.

***

The train platform was more crowded than Scott expected.

Why the hell were all these people going into New York City at ten in the morning on a weekday in August? Was there a holiday he forgot about? A 9/11 tribute he wasn't invited to? Whatever the reason, the crowd was a distraction and caused his focus to quickly crumble.

Although he was lucky enough to be sitting alone on the slatted wooden bench, the movement of people and their incessant jabbering kept forcing his attention away from the laptop sitting on his legs. For Scott, the 10:10 to Grand Central Station couldn't come soon enough.

Losers, he thought. *They have no idea that if they continue to stop me from writing, they won't be going* anywhere. *Their train will be delayed for hours until they retrieve the pieces of my body from the rails beneath them.*

It was then Scott heard loud laughter. He looked up and saw what appeared to be a group of kids in their early twenties, cackling and giggling like elementary school children. Out of the bunch of about ten, only one wasn't laughing – a handsome boy wearing a tank top, gym shorts and, strangely, a very grave expression. His physique revealed he was an athlete, and the serious expression on his face made it clear he wasn't in the same mindset as the others in his group.

As Scott tried to make out what appeared to be a school logo on the boy's shirt, a large black man passed by, obscuring his view. Scott couldn't help but follow the man, who wore clothing clearly unfitting for the intense heat of this mid-August day. The man's yellow and blue-striped tie was thrown over his shoulder, allowing his protruding belly to fill the view of anyone looking his way. His heavy beige Dockers were so wrinkled, Scott held himself back from telling the man about dry cleaners and why they exist. He cringed at the sight of armpit sweat stains spreading halfway down each side of the man's dark blue denim shirt and wondered what it was like to ...

Stop it! He yelled to himself. *Get to work, for Christ's sake.*

He returned his gaze to the laptop display, the words "Chapter One" still floating alone inside a sea of white. Placing his hands over his face, he pushed his fingers against his eyelids, hoping that would help hold back the tears of frustration. A subtle rocking of the seat made him open his eyes and look toward the end of the bench. A young man had sat down, his heels almost tucked under his butt and legs bent so tightly he buried his face in his knees. The strangest part was the knit beanie he wore, with the cuff rolled down, as though trying to hide the right side of his face.

Scott couldn't take his eyes off the man. Why the hell was he wearing a winter hat on a hot summer day? Scott shook himself loose from his stare and gazed across the tracks to the other side of the station.

This was definitely a mistake. It's not gonna work. I should've tried writing from home.

"You already tried that. For *eight months*," he muttered.

For a few seconds, he felt on the verge of losing his mind. Nothing was making sense: the thoughts in his head were jumbled, the noises around him were penetrating his skin like a million needles and he started to feel as if the people around him were walking mannequins – like he was the only living, breathing human along the entire train platform. He closed his eyes and took a deep breath, attempting to bring a sense of reality back into his body and hopefully his mind.

Nothing changed. And that, he knew, was the tipping point.

"I can't," he said aloud, not caring if anyone thought he was crazy. "You've been here over an hour and haven't written a fucking word. It's over. You know it's over." He could feel his sadness and frustration turn to anger. "Stop fooling yourself, you idiot. You're done."

Scott slammed shut the laptop, placed it next to him on the bench and slowly stood. His legs were weak and sweat poured down his back as he made his way toward the tracks, his mind almost numb as the buzzing in his head grew louder. He looked up at the clock on the station wall above the door: 10:08. Two minutes. Just two minutes until the past eight months of torture would come to an end and he could leave the world his legacy while still at the top of his game.

He inched closer to the edge of the platform, the tips of his loafers hanging over the rim. Looking down at his feet, he saw the yellow painted line, faded from years of rain and snow, its intention to ensure people's safety by warning them not to get too close to oncoming trains. Little did the line painters know their tool to save lives was just about to do the opposite.

Somewhere someone laughed. He wasn't sure if it came from within or outside his head, or if he was the one laughing. At this point, he wasn't sure of anything. All he knew for certain was that people were starting to move closer to the tracks, and as his eyes followed the rails into the distance, he could see the 10:10 turning the bend and making its way straight for the station.

The rumbling of the train grew louder as it moved into clearer focus. Scott stared at its front as though the center of the driver's cabin was a target. At that point he decided not to jump. He'd simply lean forward and let the train do the work for him. Gravity and motion would take charge and he could only hope the force of the impact would knock him out so he wouldn't feel any pain.

He looked at the clock again. 10:10. This was it. The train was about twenty seconds out. He took a deep breath and inched closer toward the platform's edge, unwittingly wobbling back and forth but keeping his balance so that when the time came, he'd be ready. Although he could barely hear anything through the chatter inside his head, the voices of the people on the platform seemed to get louder.

Are they talking about me? Do they know who I am? Will they scream when it happens?

And that's when he heard the yell.

"You crazy shit!"

Scott turned back toward the station to see a beautiful blonde woman in a bright red tee-shirt pushing her way through the crowd. Her arm was stretched out toward him, the look in her eyes revealing both compassion and horror. *If we only met two minutes ago... maybe I could've written about you... maybe I still can!* His mind was in flux as he twisted his head around and saw the train just a few feet away. He closed his eyes, unsure of which way he was leaning, when he felt a hand grab his shirt.

That was the last thing he remembered before the screams pierced his skull and everything around him went black.

CHAPTER 2

Scott pulled open the front window blinds and attempted to see through the downpour. The sky had opened up a few hours earlier and the rain refused to lighten. Worse than that, his weather app showed that the showers would continue well into the evening.

Just my luck. He had planned to walk the neighborhood, make a mental checklist of the neighbors and decide whose lives he would create havoc in. He knew it was ridiculous. Sad, really, that his imagination was so barren he couldn't simply take other people's problems and turn them into a best-selling thriller. No, he'd fallen so low he had to insert a bit of chaos into someone else's life so the story would unfold for him and hopefully write itself.

The one thing he'd promised himself from the start was that no matter what chaos he created, there would be no death or destruction. He'd add those elements later on. Right now, all he required was a person or family with some sort of discord or dilemma and offer assistance pushing the lever – gently helping that kernel expand into something he could use as the primary plot.

A pang of fear punched him in his gut. Was he really going to be able to do this? Would he be able to alter the characters enough so that the people on which the story was based wouldn't be able to figure out it really *was* based on them?

Without warning, the copyright page in all his books flashed through his mind:

This is a work of fiction. Name, characters, businesses, places, events, locales, and incidents are either the products of the author's imagination or used in a fictitious manner. Any resemblance to actual persons, living or dead, or actual events is purely coincidental.

He shut his eyes and shook his head.

This book will be a lie from the very first page. But screw it. My livelihood and reputation are at stake.

Snapping shut the blinds, he walked into the living room, plopped down on the sofa and grabbed his writing journal that sat on the glass end table. He closed his eyes so he could picture Starlight Lane and the surrounding streets. Once he had the neighborhood map inside his head, he began to list the names of all the people he knew, writing them on the page and placing a question mark beside them if he thought their lives might hold enough drama to help him create a story.

After about thirty minutes, he felt his list was complete. He tapped his pen next to each name, stopping at Joel Peterson – the gay agoraphobic who lived just three houses down from him. He'd been to Joel and Martin's home for a few get-togethers and could never quite understand the dynamic. In just about every way, Joel appeared to be normal – a typical 35-year-old IT professional who worked from home remotely fixing people's computers. The only problem was, Joel never left his house. Never. He was a handsome man with what some would call "chiseled" features, very light skin and a red birthmark of sorts, shaped like the boot of Italy, that ran from the right side of his forehead down to his earlobe. Scott deduced by the way he always tried to cover it up that the mark on his face was the reason, or at least one of the reasons, behind Joel's agoraphobia.

A few months ago, Joel and Martin had a small event at their house to help promote a local senator. Scott and Joel were in the corner of the dining room when he decided to bring up the subject of Joel's agoraphobia. At the moment he opened his mouth to ask the "why" question, Martin appeared out of nowhere and asked Scott if he wanted a refill. It was as though the man had a sixth sense and knew from across the room where the conversation was heading.

"Sure," Scott replied, even though he still had half a glass of Cabernet. "By the way, Martin, how did you and Joel meet?"

Since Martin wasn't going to let him solve the agoraphobia mystery, Scott figured he'd discover how a neurotic homebody like Joel could find a partner willing to live with someone who suffered from such a debilitating condition.

Martin, as good-looking as Joel but without the map of Italy showcased on his face, poured more wine into Scott's glass and forced a smile. "In a nutshell? We started on Tinder and ended up in love. I think that's all you need to know." He turned away with the bottle of Cabernet in hand and headed toward the other guests to offer refills.

How rude. Does he not know who I am? He must've read my books. Everyone here knows...

"Please excuse him, Scott. He's very protective of me," Joel said. He looked toward Martin pouring wine into the glass of the potential senator. "Honestly, I don't know how I got so lucky."

Me neither.

Scott placed another question mark next to Joel and Martin's names. Could he use their life as a plot? *What happens when an agoraphobic is forced to leave the security of his home? What if his partner starts playing mind games that eventually lead to Joel being forced outside? Maybe they live in a big city so when he's somehow coerced outdoors, he's surrounded by the honking of cars, the streets filled with people and the inherent bedlam of a metropolis.*

"Hmmm... definite possibility," Scott said aloud. There would be a lot more twists and turns he'd need to incorporate, but the whole "agoraphobic" thing could be a start. He crossed out the question marks and put an exclamation point beside Joel's name.

The next names on the list: Mia and Tom Blythe. *Now* there's *potential.* He looked at his watch: 12:03. Remembering it was Wednesday, Scott bolted from the sofa, ran to the closet and grabbed his umbrella. He walked outside onto the covered porch and stood beneath it, taking in a long, deep breath of rain-soaked August air. The humidity almost made him choke.

He opened his umbrella and made his way down the steps, then strolled about twenty-four feet along the cobblestone path leading to the sidewalk. Directly across the street was the entrance to Anderson Court, on which fifteen 3,000-plus-square-foot homes stood side by side, each on half- to one-acre lots.

There was rarely any activity on Anderson Court, except on Wednesdays, when an Uber, Lyft or some sort of unmarked car service would pull up to Mia and Tom's house. Since Scott typically watched the action from his front window, the only thing he could discern was a sharply dressed thirty-something, dirty blond, hedge-fund-looking dude exit the car, look suspiciously up and down the street and walk toward the Blythes' side door. After that, Scott would have no idea what happened because seven-foot hydrangeas got in the way of his field of view. But today would be different.

With a light rain still sprinkling atop his umbrella, Scott sauntered across the street. As he stepped onto the sidewalk, a black Toyota Corolla turned right off Starlight and onto Anderson Court. Scott halted in his tracks and pretended to slowly walk back toward his home. Still able to see the Blythes' home, he snatched a glance as the car slowed down and stopped in front of it.

Right on time, Mr. Hedge Fund.

The man, wearing a dark blue double-breasted suit, stepped out of the car and, as always, looked both ways as though checking for nosy neighbors. Scott pretended to continue walking home and turned just in time to see the man walk to the side of the house.

"The love entrance," Scott whispered to himself, smiling.

As he wheeled around to head back home, he heard a woman scream. Startled, he jumped and felt his heart almost leap out of his chest. "What the hell?" He darted his head in all directions, unable to determine where the scream came from.

He turned around again to check behind him. Nothing. He looked down Anderson Court. Nothing. Scott closed his eyes, as though it would help him hear better, and listened carefully. He didn't hear a thing other than the soft patter of raindrops on the wet street and a faraway rumble of thunder.

Keep calm. It's your imagination. Just like at night when it sounds like someone's trying to break in. Has anyone ever broken in? No. Just calm down.

Still unable to believe his own rationalizations, Scott ran back up the sidewalk to the cobblestone path. He dashed toward his house, leapt onto the porch, rushed through the door and slammed it shut. Leaning with his back against the door, he tried to catch his breath – and his wits.

Once his hands stopped shaking and the tightness in his stomach subsided, he crept to the wet bar and poured about two fingers of Johnnie Walker Blue. He gulped it in one swallow and poured himself another. Once he finished the second gulp, he poured himself another and brought it with him to the balcony overlooking the creek.

The clouds were beginning to separate, pulled apart by a growing breeze he could feel on the back of his sweaty neck. It sent a chill up his spine and he shivered. He took another sip of scotch, wondering if this was how he'd feel for the rest of his life: defeated, worthless, uninspired and apparently hallucinating.

He wanted to talk with someone about how he'd been feeling, but struggled to come up with a name. If he made a list of his true friends, the number would probably stop at two... one if he allowed himself to realize his financial manager, Sam, was only in his life for the money. His marriage of ten years had been a complete failure from day one. Sheila loved the author events, the parties, the fame and mostly, the fortune, but she never loved *him*. It took a while for Scott to grasp that and when he finally did, they held on another five years until she found the texts from his lover, Marie. Or was it the other one, Leah? It actually might've been Donna. But at this moment it didn't matter. He was in this alone and there was not one person he could talk to but himself — not his first choice by any stretch.

After slugging the last drop of scotch from the glass, he placed it on the table and turned back toward the creek. The sun now painted a Monet-like reflection that spanned from one side to the other. Tears welled up in Scott's eyes and he wasn't sure if they were from sadness or anger. And he didn't have the time or will to care. Pissed at himself for feeling this way, he quickly wiped his eyes before any evidence of the tears fell past the lids. There was only one way for him to feel good about life and who he had become: get back to the top of the bestseller list. The last eight months had been a fluke, they had to be. The book he was about to write would prove that to the world *and* to himself.

He thought back to what happened on the street. There was no doubt Mia was having an affair with some hot hedge-fund-manager guy who got away from the office every Wednesday for that reason and that reason only.

Now... to devise a way to create havoc.

Scott smiled, the answer as obvious as the enduring taste of scotch on his tongue. He already knew Mia's husband was a hothead. Scott had seen Tom argue politics in public with the animosity typical of a high-tempered know-nothing. He'd drink too much at block parties, his inane cackling always turning to anger and yelling over the most meaningless topics. The guy was a short-fused firecracker; the perfect victim to agitate in order to stir up trouble and create a subplot.

Scott's insides trembled with excitement.

All he had to do was have Tom find out about Mia's infidelity. Mayhem would ensue and his book would start to take shape. This was undoubtedly the perfect conflict to start establishing his premise. But now the question was: how could he get Tom to find out about the liaison? It had been going on for about a year and the putz still didn't know. How was he going to...

And then the thought slammed him like a jackhammer.

Tom had texted him a few months ago with publishing questions, something about one of his clients wanting to become a self-published author. Scott blew him off but kept the text, which meant Tom's number was somewhere on his phone. So now he had to figure out how he was going to inform Tom about Mia's tryst without being identified. He raced to his office, lifted the laptop cover and Googled "where to buy a burner phone."

The results boggled his mind. Although there were numerous places to purchase a pre-paid phone, it seemed almost impossible to make sure that any calls he made would be untraceable. Between SIM cards, triangulation, VOIP and other technological terms he couldn't pronounce, let alone comprehend, the next few hours would involve deep research. Then he'd have to wait a week before getting Tom to catch Mia and Mr. Hedge Fund in the act.

Shit. I only have fourteen days to get something to Grace. Now I'm losing a freakin' week!

It was obvious that once things got into gear, he'd have to work day and night to complete this book. But he had no choice. This was his last and only chance to make something work.

He reclined in his chair, looked out the window and silently prayed – not only that Tom would answer his call next Wednesday, but that he'd have the balls to dial Tom's number in the first place.

CHAPTER 3

Mia Blythe wore a faint smile as she gently applied the Rouge Louboutin lipstick she'd just purchased to her upper lip. She knew Dave would love it. The shade was just red enough to turn him on, yet soft enough to maintain an aura of sinlessness.

She looked at the rose on her dressing table and took a deep breath to hold back joyful tears. This was the one-year anniversary of the day they'd met, and a single rose was going to be her gift to him. It was only a few weeks after that first meeting they started their... her thought stopped... she didn't even know what to call what they had. The one thing she knew for certain was that it was one year ago today they'd seen each other for the first time and both felt something over which neither had any control. The guilt she'd felt after their initial encounter had waned over a few months as their connection grew deeper and more passionate. Although they were both married and considered their vows sacred, neither of them could stop what they'd started. They tried to call it quits more than a few times, but their attempts at staying apart were fruitless. Like iron to a magnet, they were drawn to one another both physically and emotionally, oftentimes in ways they couldn't explain – to each other or themselves.

Many times after making love, they'd lie in bed, gaze into each other's eyes and talk about when and how they would leave their spouses and spend the rest of their lives together.

Was it just talk? Will it ever really happen? She was hoping that after a year, and a freshly-picked rose, those questions would finally be answered.

Mia took one final look in the mirror. She was a bit surprised how blue her eyes appeared today, as though they had been infused with a hue of turquoise. Could it be the new lipstick? The subtle yet glittery eyeshadow? Maybe it was the soft highlights she had Toni, her hairdresser, subtly streak through her blonde hair. Whatever it was, she was confident in her looks as a thirty-six-year-old who had been through rough times and emerged smarter and stronger – weathered more on the inside than the outside.

She jumped up, took the rose from her dressing table and walked into the living room. Dave was running a bit late again, like last week when he told her he'd gotten spooked by a man with an umbrella lurking around and thought it might be Tom. He had waited in the car until the man finally turned and walked back across the street into "that author's house." Mia reassured him that Tom was hours away at a business meeting in Boston and the "lurker" was probably Scott Atwood getting some fresh air to help stir his imagination.

"In the rain?" he'd asked.

"You know those writers, they're a bit strange." She half-smiled and batted her eyelashes. "Unlike you and I who are perfectly normal in every way."

Dave's wet hair, hanging over his copper eyes, and his dark, damp suit had made him even sexier than usual. So sexy, in fact, that he was naked before they even made it to the bedroom.

But today would be different. She'd wait for the gentle tap on the side door, sit him down on the sofa, offer up the rose and let him know, in no uncertain terms, that she was in love with him. No matter his response, she'd then lead him into the bedroom and use her body to confirm exactly how she felt.

Twirling the rose stem between her fingers, Mia caught sight of a photo sitting on the fireplace mantle. It was a shot of her at the Grand Canyon, a trip she and Tom had taken when they were first married three years ago, a time when the future appeared to be bright and filled with promise. But Tom's drinking, short temper and extreme arrogance had quickly dimmed the light, and within a few months she knew she'd made a mistake. How did she not see this before they were married? Was she that stupid, or did he fool her into believing he was someone he wasn't?

Over the past year, since she'd fallen in love with Dave, just the sound of Tom's voice repulsed her. She'd recoil whenever he touched her, cringe when his car pulled into the garage. She wanted to leave, to pack her bags and call him every vile name she could think of while storming out the door. But waiting was her only option. Until she and Dave figured out a way to be together without jeopardizing their financial future or his ability to see his children, she'd have to keep pretending. And it was eating her up inside.

Just three nights ago, as she and Tom sat on the sofa watching TV, his knee touched hers ever so slightly. Mia flinched.

"Why so jumpy?" he asked.

Because your touch makes my skin crawl.

"Just a little anxious from library stuff."

Thank God she was volunteering at the library again. Late nights working at the desk or using time at home to catch up on cataloging new books had been her go-to response to spend less time with him — especially in the bedroom.

Attempting to be subtle, Tom moved closer so that his thigh fell against hers. He gently swept the hair from her neck and kissed her right below her earlobe. His stubble sent a gut-wrenching shockwave throughout her entire body.

God, no. I can't.

"I know how we can relieve some of that anxiety."

She closed her eyes and tried to think of a way out of what he wanted to do. She couldn't keep avoiding his advances without him getting suspicious. She'd have to give in every once in a while until she found a way out of this God-forsaken marriage.

"I'm not sure about..."

He grabbed her by the wrist and yanked her from the sofa as though she was an old, ragged quilt cover.

"For Christ's sake, you're never sure. But guess what?" He was now walking so quickly, it felt as if he dragged her into the bedroom. "I'm sure."

When they reached the bedroom, he pushed her down onto the mattress. Her heart was pounding so hard, she feared it would burst out of her chest. As Tom unbuckled his belt, she tried to speak but no sound escaped. She rolled herself off the side of the bed, stood straight up and swallowed hard.

"You're sure?" she asked, her voice trembling. *Be careful.* "You're sure? About what, Tom? Are you going to rape me? Tell me, what the hell are you *sure* about?"

He stopped short of pulling down his pants and glared at her with a stunned expression. Mia could see the rage in his eyes, the flush enveloping his face. He bit his lip and attempted a deep breath.

"Don't make me..." Although he tried to contain his fury, she could hear it bubbling deep within his voice.

"Make you what?"

He crossed his arms and twisted his head toward the door as though someone had just walked in. He turned back to her.

"What the fuck, Mia? It's been like three weeks. What's the problem? Don't you like sex anymore? You on your period again? Are you a lesbian? I mean really, what the hell is your problem?"

At that moment, the only thought running through Mia's mind was a vision of Dave bursting through the front door, grabbing her by the hand and helping her escape from this lunatic. But she knew it was a fantasy, a dream... at least for now.

She faked a laugh. "Yes, Tom. I'm a lesbian."

"You might as well be. I mean, I'm your husband and you barely let me touch you."

"So, what, you're going to take from me what I don't give you?"

A bead of sweat dripped down Tom's left temple. He uncrossed his arms and flexed his fingers open and closed as though he were getting ready for a boxing match.

Mia waited for a response.

Nothing.

"How about you treat me with some respect and show a little tenderness? I might have a different reaction."

Tom took a deep breath and Mia watched his mood shift from rage to what appeared to be despair. For a split second she felt pity for him, then tossed it aside as quickly as it hit her. She was in this position because he dragged her into the bedroom and threw her on the bed. And she was going to pity *him?* Not gonna happen.

He zipped his pants and slowly walked toward her. Mia planted her feet firmly into the carpet, unsure whether she'd need to stand her ground after he slapped her across the face or assaulted her with his hands. When Tom finally reached her, he gently put his arms around her and pulled her close. He didn't apologize in words. He never did. For Tom, acting vulnerable was the closest he'd ever gotten to an apology.

When he stopped hugging her, he stood back and looked into her eyes and then at her lips. *I will not let him kiss me. Anything but a kiss.* She turned her head away and closed her eyes, trying to hold back tears as his hands hungrily grabbed every inch of her body. Trying to detach her thoughts from the moment, she thought of Dave and their life together. No matter how repulsed she was, she knew she had to give in to what was about to happen. Her future depended on it.

The tap on the side door snapped her out of the sickening memory and back into the present moment. Dave was here and that was the only thing she'd focus on. A flush came over her, almost as though this was her first high school date. She smelled the rose, straightened her blouse and headed for the door with a feeling deep inside that this would be a day she'd never forget.

***

When Dave handed Mia a rose, she broke down in tears.

He pulled her close, held her face to his chest and stroked her hair while kissing the top of her head. "Why are you crying?"

Through her sobs, her voice could barely utter the words she wanted to say. "You remembered."

Dave laughed. "Of course I remembered." He took her hand, the one holding the rose she was about to give him, and smiled. "Looks like you remembered, too."

She sniffled and hugged him tighter.

He led her to the chaise lounge section of the couch and leaned back with her against it. Mia smelled the rose and used her shirt hem to dab the tears falling down her cheeks.

"I don't even want to know what my mascara looks like," she mumbled.

Dave placed his finger beneath her chin and delicately lifted her face toward his. "It looks beautiful. Like two very narrow creeks of black oil." He wiped both streaks with his thumb. "More beautiful than ever," he whispered.

Mia kissed him and closed her eyes, the softness of his lips almost drowning her thoughts. As hard as it was, she pulled herself away and looked directly into his emerald irises.

"I'm in love with you." She looked down to the sofa cushion, unsure whether or not she wanted to hear a response.

A few seconds passed. Mia was about to tell him he didn't need to respond when he placed a hand on each side of her face and gently raised her head so she'd be looking at him again.

"As I am with you," he whispered back.

"How are we going to – "

He placed his index finger over her lips. "Shhh, babe, we're going to work this out. This weekend, while the kids are sleeping over at my parent's house, I'm going to have the talk with Sue. It's over with her. It has been for years and she knows it. Honestly, I think she'll be as relieved as I'll be." Dave turned toward the photo on the fireplace mantel. "The question is, when will you tell Tom, and do you want me there when you do?"

Mia fingered the rose petals. *So soft. So delicate.* They reminded her of Dave's lips. "I'll do it this weekend, too. I'll have my bags in the car, tell him I just can't do it anymore and I'll leave."

Dave helped her up from the sofa and put his hands around her waist. "I'll figure out a place to meet after we've both had our talks with them. I'll text it to you tonight or tomorrow, okay?"

"Yes." The sound of her own assent surprised her, then thrilled her deeply. "*Yes.*" It was going to happen.

Her heart pounded with both fear and excitement. She didn't know what Tom's reaction would be when she told him she was leaving, but she'd be sure to be near the front door in case he went after her. She'd also have some kind of weapon in her hand. He was too unpredictable and she'd have to plan everything down to the most minute detail.

For right now, though, she had the love of her life standing right in front of her and she didn't want to waste another moment with negative thoughts. She kissed him on the mouth and when her tongue met his, she felt chills run down her spine. Dave took her by the hand and led her toward the bedroom.

"Our future begins now," he said quietly.

Mia smiled and kissed his hand. *Our future began the moment we met.*

CHAPTER 4

It took Scott three tries before he was finally able to press "dial" on the burner phone. He'd been going back and forth all morning: *Should I? Shouldn't I? Should I? Shouldn't I?* Over and over the words echoed in his head. He didn't know if he was losing his mind or his courage.

Even though he'd made the final decision last night that calling Tom was the only way to save his career, the thought of what he was about to do made his insides cringe, almost to the point of vomiting. But he didn't have a choice; his creative vault held nothing but smoking ashes and he was counting on the aftermath of this phone call to help turn those cinders into flames.

As he paced the length of the living room windows waiting for Tom to answer, a wave of panic hit and he thought about hanging up. *Take a breath. Just breathe.* He held a thin dish towel over the phone's speaker to disguise his voice, just in case Tom recognized it from the few times they'd met.

"This is Tom," the voice said. Scott panicked and couldn't speak. Trying to clear his throat, he walked away from the window as though that would help keep him from getting caught.

"Hello?" Tom said. "Hello?" Scott was about to respond when he heard the blaring of a car horn. "Get out of the left lane you asshole! What a stupid piece of shit. What the hell is wrong with..." Tom abruptly ended his tirade. "Hello? Who is this?"

Scott shook his head like a football kicker running toward the field, attempting to rid himself of all thought as if his career depended on this one field goal.

"Go home," Scott mumbled. He was so shocked by the sound of his own voice that his hand holding the phone started to tremble.

"What? Who is this?"

"You'd better get home," Scott said, more loudly this time. "Now!"

"Who the hell is this? What's going on?"

"It doesn't matter. Just get home and find out for yourself!"

"Did you do something to Mia? Are you with her now? Who the fu...?"

Scott pulled the phone from his ear, looked at the display and tapped the red button to hang up. He kept his eyes on the screen to make certain the call had ended. With his hands still trembling, he removed the SIM card from the phone, ran to the bathroom, threw it down the toilet and flushed three times. From there, he took the phone and placed it in a plastic bag he had left on the kitchen counter. He then moved into the garage, set the bag on the ground, grabbed the rubber mallet hanging on the wall and smashed the phone until the tiny bits of it inside the bag were indiscernible. As though the bag was filled with a poisonous substance, Scott picked it up by the corners, pinching each with two fingers, and buried it within the garbage that packed the close-to-full garbage pail. He wiped the sweat from his brow, relieved by the fact that the rubbish would be picked up tomorrow and thrown into obscurity among the tons of waste already polluting the city dump.

His body was still in panic mode. Scott hurried back into the living room and began pacing again, trying to rid himself of the stress that had completely overtaken him. His breathing was heavy, as though he'd just sprinted across town. *What did I do? Am I crazy? Who the hell would do something like this?*

"A lunatic, that's who," he said aloud. "You've lost your fucking mind. You know that, right?"

Or have I? I could be the lead character in the book I'm writing – the antagonist everyone loves to hate. The despicable genius working behind the scenes that no one suspects of any wrong doing until...

From out of the blue, a sharp pain pierced his upper right arm and he grabbed it with his left hand. *What the hell?* He rubbed and massaged it until the pain eventually became a dull ache. At first he feared it was a heart attack until he realized if it was, he'd have felt the pain in his left arm. *Idiot. It's just nerves... tension... stress. Let it go.*

Still holding his arm, he walked out to the front porch and halfway down the cobblestone path. If Tom was in his car when he received Scott's call, he could've been ten or a hundred miles away.

There was no telling when he'd show up - if he showed up at all. Scott continued to walk anxiously down the path toward the street, hoping with every step that all would stay as calm as it was at that very moment and Tom would never appear. Maybe there was another way to come up with an idea for the book. Something less... less... mischievous.

He glanced down both sides of the street. Other than a semi-amorphous figure walking a dog way down at the end of Starlight, there was nothing to see. Not one car. Not one other person. Not even one of those chipmunks that were always scurrying in front of his feet. Scott started to relax a bit. It was still too soon for him to replace his worry with relief, but it had been at least ten minutes since he'd made the call and Tom still hadn't shown up. If Mia's husband was *that* concerned about his wife, he would've called the cops and they'd be banging down the door by now.

The more time that passed, the more Scott's nerves unwound. He wondered what Grace would think if she knew what he'd done. Knowing her, she'd probably yell "kudos!" and offer him a high-five. She wouldn't care what he had to do to get a book out, as long as she got her commission and could easily afford her next Bahama vacation.

Then Sheila came to mind. God, she'd be so disappointed in him. Not like that was anything new. She never gave him credit for his work, his achievements. No credit for anything. Nothing was ever enough for her. He should have realized that was going to be his future during their first sexual encounter. Rather than telling him what she wanted, she told him everything he was doing wrong. Jesus Christ, how did he end up marrying the one person who...

At first the noise sounded like a bee buzzing from way off in the distance. Within seconds, the droning grew into a soft roar and he looked down the road to see a car heading directly toward him.

Holy shit, it's Tom.

Panic-stricken, Scott could only run up the path to his house, hop the steps to the porch and rush inside.

After slamming the door shut, he peeked out the blinds and saw Tom's Lexus barely slow down as it made the right onto Anderson Court. Scott's legs went weak as spaghetti. It was like a dream, a movie, as though someone else had made that phone call and he was watching the effects of *their* actions.

In disbelief he watched the Lexus grind to a halt in front of Mia's house, the skidding tires creating a smokescreen behind the car. Scott gasped when Tom opened the door and exited the car with a gun in his hand. He wanted to run outside and up the block to stop Tom and tell him it was all a big mistake. But then he'd give himself away. He turned from the window and faced the living room. He turned around again, unable to stop himself from watching what was about to unfold.

Holy shit! What should I do? What the hell do I do now?

He used two fingers to separate the blinds and peek out into the street. Tom was heading toward the front door and suddenly disappeared behind the tall hydrangeas lining the driveway. Scott shook his head in disbelief. It was too late to do anything now but pray.

His legs still weak and the pain in his arm more severe than ever, he fell into his desk chair and laid his head on his hands. His emotions were running a thousand miles an hour and he wasn't sure whether he was about to scream or sob.

His regret over what he'd done overwhelmed him and he had to put a stop to it. He found the strength to stand up, walk to the front door and, with numb legs, make his way down the porch steps and up the cobblestone path. He stopped at the sidewalk's edge to make sure no cars were coming. As he placed one foot into the street, he heard the bang – so loud, Scott fell to the curb. It was definitely a gunshot, the same sound he'd heard over and over at the range while researching firearm kickback for *Don't Be Fooled*.

Oh my God, no! No! Holy shit, this can't be happening! Oh, Jesus, please don't...

As he prayed to a deaf God, he saw Tom stagger across the street toward his car, get inside and take off so quickly, the screech of the tires forced Scott to place his hands over his ears, closing his eyes. The darkness behind the lids joined sudden silence as the engine's buzz faded away, but neither soothed him.

When he finally looked back up, the car had disappeared and a cloud of smoke from the burning tires lingered in its place. Inside his head, Scott heard police car sirens and the sound of people yelling and screaming. And yet, when he glanced up and down the street, there were no police cars, no screaming people. It was as empty as it had been ten seconds earlier.

Holy shit, I really am losing my mind. Where are the screams coming from? The sirens? Are non-existing sounds a side effect of guilt? But I'm not guilty. Tom's guilty. I didn't shoot anyone. Tom did. Or did he?

He pulled himself up and stumbled back across the path and into his house. He slammed the door and stood in the hallway. After about five minutes of what felt like an eternity, he heard the sound of police sirens. Real sirens, not from inside his head but from up the street. From the window alongside the front door, he could see the cop cars speeding toward the Blythes'. He watched as the cops exited their vehicles, cocked their weapons and crept toward the house.

Scott could no longer bear to watch. He shivered and struggled to make his way to the sofa. The pain in his arm was subsiding as a wave of dizziness enveloped his entire head. He didn't even want to imagine what happened inside Mia's house. *Who was shot? Are they both dead? Did Tom kill his own wife?*

Scott slumped back on the sofa pillow, leaned over and let his face fall in the crack between the cushion and the arm of the sofa. Soon enough he'd find out what kind of devastation and grief he'd caused, and have to live with regret for the rest of his life. Most importantly, he'd have to hold his breath waiting to see if everything he'd done would help his career.

In the meantime, he pushed his face into the sofa and, for no apparent reason he could think of, sobbed uncontrollably until he finally lost consciousness.

***

Detective Darryl Jordan leaned forward in the chair and placed an elbow on each knee. He hoped moving closer to Mia would help him better understand her unintelligible responses to his questions. As he had entered the house, the attending officers warned him she'd been mumbling from the moment they arrived and found her sobbing over the victim's lifeless body. But she was in worse shape than he had imagined.

Once he made it to the scene and finally persuaded Mia to leave the bedroom, he gently helped her sit down in one of the oversized living room chairs. She curled up there like a frightened puppy, clad in her lover's oversized dress shirt and a pair of skimpy black shorts. Her feet were tucked beneath her tiny frame and her lips moved as though she was saying something, but only silence came from them.

"Mrs. Blythe," Jordan said softly, to no response. "Mrs. Blythe," he repeated, a little louder. Mia just stared at her knee, picking at it with her fingernails as though there was a stubborn piece of peeling skin that wouldn't come loose. *Final try before I call in a shrink.* "Mia!" Jordan yelled this time. She looked up, her face without expression, black trails of mascara smeared across each cheek.

"Yes," she said, almost under her breath.

"Again, I'm Detective Jordan." He used his notepad to point to the man sitting beside him. "And this is Detective Halleran. We know this is a very, very rough time for you. We just need to know what happened here today so we can make this right for you and your..." Jordan gestured toward the bedroom. He gave a side-glance to Halleran and cleared his throat. "Do you think you can help us with that, Mrs. Blythe?"

"Mia," she said. "Don't use that last name with me ever again. My name is Mia!" Her voice was now a little *too* loud. He'd hit a nerve and knew he had to back off before the situation got out of hand.

"Okay, Mia. Please, calm down. I understand you're in shock right now and that this all seems, well, surreal. We just want your take on what happened so we can get to the bottom of this."

Mia stopped picking at her knee and crossed her legs, Indian-style. She swept back the hair hanging over her eyes and clasped her hands together. "You want to know what happened? I'll tell you what happened." She pointed to the Grand Canyon photo over the fireplace. "That piece of shit killed the love of my life." Her head fell forward again and she let her hair descend over her eyes. "Shot him, right in the chest... killed him... the love of my life... just pointed the gun at him and..." Her voice started to fade.

Jordan moved closer to her chair. "Mia!" He didn't want to intimidate her, but he would do whatever it took to keep her focused and get the entire story – for her sake, as well as his. "Stay with me." He looked at the photo, then back to Mia. "Who's that man in the photo with you?"

"Tom, my husband," Mia responded, her voice vacant of emotion. "Soon to be *ex*-husband."

Jordan and Halleran shot a glance at one another.

"Okay," Halleran said, placing his pen onto his notepad, ready to write. "So who's the man in the bedroom?"

Mia started to cry and used the cuffs of the man's shirt she was wearing to wipe her eyes. Halleran grabbed the box of tissues from the side table, pulled one out and handed it to her. Then he placed the box on the arm of Mia's chair. Jordan could tell Halleran was getting annoyed and flashed him a look that insisted he chill out. This was no time for good cop, bad cop.

"Dave," Mia cried. "That's my Dave." She mopped her nose with tissues. "Today was our one-year anniversary. This weekend he was going to tell his wife and I was going to tell Tom that we wanted to spend the rest of our lives together. But..." Mia looked up to the ceiling and closed her eyes. The tears wouldn't stop flowing. "But that's never going to happen now. Tom took it away from us. Took it all away. The way he takes *everything* away."

"Okay, let me get this straight, Mia," Halleran started. "You're currently married to Tom Blythe. You were in an intimate relationship with David Moore, who is also married. Your husband caught the two of you together, while... in the bedroom. He then shot Mr. Moore. Is that correct?"

Mia nodded.

"Can you just tell me the exact series of events? If you tell me –"

"What else do you need to know, for Christ's sake?" Mia's voice rose into a yell, surprisingly clear. "You just said it all, plain and simple. Why do I need to go over it again and again?"

Halleran let out a sigh and leaned his back against the sofa. He looked to Jordan for help, who just raised his eyebrows and offered a subtle shrug.

That's what you get for being an asshole to a woman in pain.

Jordan knew that Halleran was still pissed about his promotion to Detective last year; he'd heard him in the locker room at the station talking about how Collins should've been promoted instead, but because of all the "diversity bullshit" in the department, they promoted a black man instead. Never mind that Jordan was top of his class at Columbia or that he'd spent the last five years as a low-level officer trying to enforce the law on the street. Halleran was more concerned with the politics of Scarsdale than the citizens who lived there, and it was evident in his attitude toward Jordan.

He decided not to play Halleran's game. Holding back any dirty looks or snide remarks, he turned away from his "partner" and edged closer toward Mia.

"Mia, I'll be honest. I don't want to have to bring you down to the station for questioning." Her eyes widened and it looked like the waterworks were about to restart. He tried to stop that from happening by quickly saying, "And I won't have to do that if you can just walk me through what happened from the time you saw Tom until the moment your neighbor Mrs. Camino called 9-1-1 and the police entered your house." Wanting to offer comfort, but uncertain of what reaction reaching out to touch her would produce, Jordan placed his hand on the arm of her chair. "By the way, is there anyone we can call for you? Family? A friend? Someone who can be with you?"

Mia shook her head.

"No. No one. I have a sister in Minnesota I don't speak to anymore. And I really don't have many friends." She shook her head harder. "No... I really can't think of anyone to call."

She sounded bereft, not surprisingly, but with several complete sentences from her mouth Jordan felt her lucidity was gradually returning.

"Okay," Jordan said. "Then just go through what happened, step by step, and I promise we'll take care of getting you the help you need."

Mia dabbed her eyes with tissues and sniffled.

"Dave and I were in the bedroom when I heard a noise. It sounded like a click. That's when I heard Tom yell my name. He yelled it over and over again. Dave sat up. I think he said something about getting dressed. I'm not sure." Her voice began to tremble.

Halleran jumped in. "It's okay, Mia. Take a breath. Just take a breath and continue when you're ready."

Oh, look at that, Jordan thought, *the man might actually have feelings.* But that thought quickly changed when memories of Halleran's past swept before his mind's eye – the multiple occasions he'd use his lady-killing good looks to pretend to help other beautiful grieving women recover from their loss. Like a corrupt realtor reading the obits for leads, Halleran slithered around mournful women until he'd seal the deal or they'd pushed him away. Yeah, he'd done it before and there was something telling Jordan he was doing it again, this time analyzing Mia to see if she might be another potential conquest. Jordan closed his eyes, attempting to wipe the loathsome yet very plausible suspicion from his thoughts.

Mia obeyed Halleran by taking a big breath and exhaling slowly. She shook her head, as if trying to regain her senses. "Dave was reaching down to the floor, like he was trying to grab his pants or shirt. I'm not sure. Tom was standing at the end of the bed pointing the gun at... I'm not even sure which one of us he was pointing the gun at. First he pointed it at me. Then at Dave. Then at me again. It was like he couldn't make up his mind."

Mia stopped speaking. She glanced at Halleran, then back at Jordan. It was apparent she didn't want to continue. Jordan blinked slowly and nodded his head in a gesture that said, *It's okay, just keep going.*

Mia looked up at the ceiling—another attempt to keep the tears from forming, Jordan thought. It didn't work.

"For seconds, minutes, I really can't remember, none of us moved. Tom just stood there staring at us both. I stared back and without looking away, I tried to find Dave's hand. That's when Dave went to stand up and Tom..." She started to sob and held her face in her hands. "After that" – she was almost choking – "I just remember screaming and yelling. Dave was pleading and then there was the shot. He fell back on the bed and I just kept screaming." She lowered her hands. Her eyes were swollen, the rims a dark crimson. "The next thing I remember after that was the police coming into the room. I swear, I don't remember anything else. Not even Tom leaving."

Halleran scribbled on his pad and blew out a sigh.

"Did you even *think* about calling 9-1-1?" he asked.

"The only thing I was thinking about was how to turn back time. I could tell Dave was gone. 9-1-1 couldn't have done anything for him. I just wanted to hold him. That's all. Just hold him."

Out of the corner of his eye, Jordan saw two associates from the coroner's office exiting the bedroom door. They made certain Mia was facing the other way before wheeling Dave's body, now inside a shiny black body bag atop the gurney, toward the front door. Jordan pointed to the Grand Canyon photo on the fireplace mantle to help keep her attention off what was happening.

"How long ago was that taken?"

She looked at the photo. "Three years ago."

"Were you happy back then? You look happy."

"Fake happy. I was always fake happy. I'm tired of being fake happy."

Halleran shifted in his chair and smirked. Jordan eyed him. *Did you get your answer? You gonna try to make her happy now you rotten, son of a...*

"Any other questions you want to ask, detective?" Halleran asked, pushing his palms against his knees and standing up.

Jordan squinted, surprised by Halleran's question. *He must know I'm onto him.* "No. Nothing I can think of at the moment."

Jordan finished his notes and glanced around the room to make sure everyone was doing their job. Forensics was still in the bedroom and the team was dusting for fingerprints. He looked toward the front door, where he could see two officers keeping the press at bay.

Mia turned her head toward the bedroom. Jordan watched her eyes as they grew larger and a pained expression crossed her face.

"How long will these people be here?" she asked.

Jordan slipped his pad into the inside of his suit jacket. "They should be done soon."

She attempted to jump up from the chair but fell backward. Jordan rose and positioned himself next to her in case she tried to stand up again. It was obvious that her legs were too weak to hold her up. "Dave!" she exclaimed. "What about Dave? I need to..."

This time Jordan placed his hand gently on her shoulder.

"It's okay. We're taking care of him. He's on his way to the coroner's office. We'll talk in a day or two about how you want to handle things. His wife will probably have a say in what happens to –"

"I can't stay here," she interrupted. "I can't go back in that room. I can't be here alone."

"I understand," Jordan said. He turned to ask Halleran about getting in touch with victim intervention, but his partner was already making his way out the front door. "That's why I'd like to find someone you might be able to stay with. If not, we have people who work with survivors of crisis situations just like this. I can –"

"Joel," she interrupted again. "Joel Peterson. He's a friend who lives up the block, over on Starlight Lane. I don't know why I didn't think of him before. I can stay with him."

Jordan cleared his throat. "Starlight? Does he live by Scott Atwood?"

"Yes, three houses down from him." Mia tilted her head. "You know Scott?"

Jordan gave a negligible shrug and cracked a slight smile. "Yeah, I've consulted with him on a few of his books. Once in a while we..."

"Can I call him now?" Mia interrupted.

"Scott Atwood?" Jordan asked, a bit surprised by her request.

"No, Joel. Can I call Joel?"

"Of course," Jordan responded, feeling oddly disappointed by her lack of interest in his relationship with a famous author. "Where's your cell phone?"

She twisted a few strands of hair as though that would help her recall where she'd left it.

"I'm not sure. It could be in the kitchen. Maybe the bathroom. It might be in the..." She wouldn't allow herself to turn toward the bedroom. "It might be..."

"I'll find it." Jordan quickly stood and began walking toward the bedroom when he saw a phone sitting on the kitchen counter. He grabbed it and held it up. "Is this it?"

Mia nodded, now tugging on those strands of hair.

Jordan handed her the phone and sat back down on the sofa. "If it works out, we'll have an unmarked car sit in front of Joel's house until we find Tom and take him into custody."

Before he finished his sentence, Mia was already standing in the corner of the living room talking with Joel, her head turned toward the wall. Jordan tried to hear what she was saying, but her whispering made it apparent she wanted the conversation to remain secret. He rechecked his notes until she finished her call, slowly stood and walked back over to her.

"I can bring you to Joel's house, Mia. Are there a few things you'd like to pack? Certain items you'd like to take with you?"

She was about to walk into the bedroom when she stopped short, almost falling forward.

"I can't go in there," she said, walking instead into the kitchen to grab her wallet and keys. "I just can't."

"Do you have an overnight bag or suitcase anywhere?" Jordan asked.

"In the hall closet." Mia stood at the kitchen sink, splashing water on her face. "My laptop is in the bedroom, too. Can you pack that also?"

Jordan grabbed the bag from the closet and handed it to the only uniformed cop still in the house.

"Of course," he replied. "Officer, please take this bag and throw in some clothes, undergarments, and whatever she might need for a few days, including the laptop. I have a feeling she won't be back here for a while."

Jordan walked into the kitchen and waited for Mia to finish drying her face with a paper towel.

"What about Tom?" she asked, throwing the paper towel into the garbage. "Is he in jail yet?" Her voice rose in pitch and volume. "I want him to rot in prison for the rest of his life." Her voice began quivering on the words and had become so faint, Jordan could barely hear her when she whimpered, "He's the one who should be dead."

Obviously, she hadn't heard a word he said about having protection outside her friend Joel's house. Jordan placed his hand on her shoulder. "I get it, Mia. I get it. We have people out looking for him now. He hasn't been seen since he left here. We'll find him. I promise. And we'll bring him to justice." He took her other shoulder and forced her to look at him so she'd hear what he was about to say. "As I said before, we're going to have an unmarked car in front of Joel's house just in case Tom decides to try to find you. Okay?"

Mia shook her head.

The crowd outside the house was getting louder, and Jordan wondered how he'd get her to Joel's house without having to fight their way through the press and nosy neighbors. Though the yellow crime scene tape had cordoned everyone off a safe distance from the house, reaching Starlight would mean passing through the tape and the mass of people behind it. "Mia, is there any way to get to your friend Joel's without going out the front door?"

Mia thought for a few seconds. "We can go out the back and cut through the break in the hedges that leads to the Currans' backyard. Then we can go to the other side of their lot, walk to the front and we'll almost be at the end of the street. That's only a few houses away from Joel on Starlight."

"Perfect," he said. He took the suitcase from the officer's hand and murmured in his ear. "In exactly three minutes, two-way Halleran and tell him to let the press know that Mia is out of the house and if they want an update, they should meet me down at the station."

"Got it, detective. Three minutes," the officer repeated.

Jordan struggled to see in front of them. The sun had retreated hours ago and the corner of Mia's backyard was pitch black. He turned on his phone's flashlight and found the break in the hedges. He followed Mia in silence as she made her way across the Currans' backyard – a yard, he figured, that was three times the size of his own house. At the edge of the brick patio, she made a left and then a quick right.

They were now on the front lawn of the neighbors two houses down from Mia, facing Anderson Court, about forty feet from

Starlight Lane. He looked to the left and could see the crowd dispersing and the press heading into their vans. Jordan grabbed Mia's arm. Until the press had completely disappeared, Mia wouldn't be safe from some sort of media harassment.

"Let's move. I don't want them to catch up with us."

They ran to the end of the block, crossed over Starlight and hurried to Joel's house. On the way up the slight incline to the front door, he glanced behind him to make sure no one had followed them. The darkness was empty, the street behind them just as clear.

When they reached the door, a young man – Joel, Jordan assumed – held it open. A dark hoodie covered most of his face, but Jordan quickly caught a look of concern that made him feel slightly envious. *She's lucky to have someone with such compassion.* Mia fell into the man's arms and began to sob. He hugged her tightly and let her nestle her tear-soaked face into the crook of his neck. He gestured for Jordan to hand him the overnight bag, which he did immediately.

"I got this," he whispered to the detective and gently closed the door.

Jordan turned around and gazed at the black, star-filled sky. The only movement came from the blinking lights of an airplane moving silently across the night, a smoky gray contrail streaking in its wake.

"I hope so," he said to no one. "I really do."

CHAPTER 5

The persistent ringing of the doorbell jolted Scott into consciousness.

He was still face down on the sofa, his stiff neck proof that he must've been lying in that same position all night. The bell continued to ring as he pulled himself up and headed to the front door, dragging his feet the entire way. Like the firing of an air pistol, yesterday's events thrust themselves into his head and a wave of dizziness forced him to lean against the wall.

Holy shit. What the hell did I do?

Scott looked at the wall clock hanging in the dining room. The pendulum swung slowly, making his head spin that much more. It was just past 8:30 AM. *Fifteen hours? How did I sleep for fifteen hours? That's not possible. I...*

The doorbell rang again, making him jump. He stood up straight and glanced into the mirror on the wall to his left. His hair looked like a mohawk, flat on both sides and sticking up in the middle. As he neared the door, he pushed down his hair and tried to fluff out the sides.

"Who is it?" he yelled, grabbing the door handle.

"Scarsdale Police," a male voice answered.

"It's me, too, Scott. Darryl Jordan."

Scott slumped over, holding onto the door handle without pushing it down. Although he was friendly with Jordan, who over many a cocktail had helped him with some police procedural details for his last few novels, Scott was hesitant to open the door. What did they know? Why were they here? What did they want from him? His heart was beating so fast he thought he might pass out. He took a deep breath and closed his eyes until his pulse slowed a bit and he felt strong enough to stand up straight.

When he opened the door, he saw Jordan first and forced a smile.

"Hey, Darryl," Scott said, reaching out his hand.

Darryl shook it, his troubled expression showing reluctance at displaying their personal relationship. It was obvious he wanted to keep that under wraps.

Turning toward the man beside Jordan, Scott squinted. The sun was behind the two men, hot and blinding, the beginning of a scorching, humid day, the kind of weather Scott hated the most. It made their features difficult to make out, but as an author, Scott knew how to find detail in even the most undefined images. The man with Jordan had black, slicked-back hair, dark blue eyes and a persistent frown that must have created those two perpendicular crevasses between his brow. Scott immediately disliked him and rolled his eyes at Jordan as the other man scoured his notepad.

"This is Detective John Halleran," Jordan said, glancing toward the man beside him.

Halleran finally looked up at Scott and nodded.

Scott returned the nod and carefully studied both men, searching for an opportunity to distract them from the true reason for their visit. He noticed that both their necks were moist with sweat.

"It's a thousand degrees out there," Scott said. "And you're both wearing ties. Seriously?"

"Protocol," Halleran muttered.

"Well, what's going on? Do you want to come in and cool off for a few minutes?"

Please say "no." Please say "no."

"We can't." Jordan sounded disappointed. "We have quite a few houses to get to. I think we'd –"

"Mr. Atwood," Halleran started. He sounded annoyed, as if the relationship between Scott and Jordan did not meet with his approval. He again glanced at his notepad. "One of your neighbors, Karen Camino, said that you work from home. Is that correct?"

"Yes." Scott wasn't offering up anything else. Karen was the neighborhood gossip and for whatever reason, she didn't like him. He wasn't sure if it was his personality or his books she detested, but either way, he was angry that she took it upon herself to share his work habits with the cops. He'd be sure to figure out how to get his revenge on her big mouth, but in the meantime, he had to deal with the problem at hand.

"Well, I'm sure you saw all the commotion that went on yesterday," Halleran said, attempting to regain his attention. "And I'm also sure you've seen the news."

Scott turned his head side to side and then straight toward Anderson Court, where he saw a single police car and one press van.

"To be honest, I was in my office writing all day long. Non-stop." The detectives kept watching him, obviously expecting more. "I wear noise-canceling headphones with meditative music that uses binaural beats. Kind of puts me in a trance while I write. I wouldn't know if there was a nuclear explosion."

The detectives shared an expression of disappointment. Then Halleran turned to Scott and tilted his head as though confused. "Were you writing when we rang the bell?"

On the inside, Scott panicked. On the outside, he didn't change the look on his face, nor did he alter his tone of voice.

"I'm embarrassed to say that I passed out on the couch last night." He pointed to his hair. "As you can see, I pretty much woke up as you were ringing the bell. So I haven't seen the news either." Scott again squinted as though trying to see up the block. "So what happened? What's going on? Why are you here?"

"Well, you'll find out sooner or later –" Jordan began.

Halleran interrupted. "So, you're saying you didn't see or hear anything that went on around here yesterday?"

Scott shook his head.

"Absolutely nothing?" Halleran tried again.

"No, I'm sorry. I get into writing mode and with my headphones and the music, I'm like dead to the world."

Halleran jotted something on his pad.

"Can you just tell me what happened? Is anyone hurt?"

Halleran kept writing while he turned to Jordan and nodded as though giving permission for him to provide information. Scott could see Jordan's jaw muscles tighten as he ground his teeth.

"It's the Blythes'," Jordan said. "There was a shooting." His expression turned mournful. "I can't get into detail right now, but one person is dead. We're searching for the husband, Tom Blythe, and trying to find someone who might've seen him."

Scott shook his head, worried they'd see his heart pounding through his tee-shirt. "Oh my God! Mia! How is Mia?"

Halleran stopped writing. "Do you know her? Personally?"

"I know them both from neighborhood events – fundraisers and the like. I don't *know* them, know them. But I know them well enough to be concerned. Is Mia okay?"

"Yes," Jordan said. "Physically she's okay, but mentally she's under a lot of stress."

Scott was about to ask more questions when Halleran flipped closed his pad. "That's it for now, Mr. Atwood," he said. "We appreciate all of your help."

The sarcasm slapped Scott across his face. "You're welcome," he slapped back.

Jordan watched Halleran walk down the porch steps and waited until he was out of earshot.

"I'll call you when I get a minute. Right now, we're on the hunt for Tom Blythe and I'm not sure where it's going to lead."

Scott smiled. "I get it. I swear, if I hear anything from anyone, I'll call you first."

Jordan offered him a thumbs-up and turned around, wiping the back of his neck with a handkerchief he'd pulled from his back pocket. When he reached Halleran, they shared a few words, made their way to the sidewalk and turned right.

Scott let out the breath he'd been holding since the moment he opened the door. When he reentered the house, he gently closed the door, leaned with his back up against it and slid down until his butt hit the floor. He laid his arms on his knees and gazed straight through the living room and out the huge windows to the forest of trees and handful of giant homes lining the other side of the creek.

He felt electrical surges trickle down his spine. The jarring realization that he was responsible for another person's death began gnawing at his insides like a dog on a bone. But he stopped it mid-bite.

Not my problem, he thought. *There's nothing I can do. It's done.*

He knew there wasn't anything he could take back, no action that could return his life and the lives of his neighbors back to the way they were. Mr. Hedge Fund was dead and there was a manhunt in the works to find Tom, now probably the town's most wanted maniac, lunatic, and murderer.

Scott almost choked on the irony that he was as responsible as Tom, if not more, of being all of those things.

***

Using his shoulder to hold the cellphone to his ear, Joel Peterson popped a Xanax in his mouth and downed it with a slug of water from his Poland Spring bottle. He knew his doctor would be pissed that he'd taken the Xanax after just starting the Paxil, but Joel had no choice. His panic was out of control.

Joel had called Martin, hoping he'd be able to keep him from hiding under the covers or locking himself in the bathroom like the old days. But Martin's soothing words and tone weren't working this time. *Maybe it's the Paxil. Maybe it's making it worse. Maybe I should...*

"Joel... babe, are you listening?"

"To what, Martin? To you telling me there's nothing to worry about? That I should keep calm and breathe? I pay a shrink two hundred dollars a week to tell me that through my computer." Joel took a breath and shook his head, trying to release the panic attack "demons," as he called them. "I saw the police through the side window. They're going house to house, probably asking questions about yesterday."

"I know. You told me that already. But again, you don't know anything. There's no reason for them to make you leave the house. You were working, heard a bang and that's all you know."

Joel paced the corridor leading from the front door to the great room. Back and forth... back and forth. He had taken off his shoes and socks to ensure his anxiety march wouldn't wake Mia and now his sweaty bare feet were sticking to the wood floor. He hoped the odd sound they made as they peeled off the wide maple planks wouldn't stir her from sleep.

"Joel? Do you hear what I'm saying?"

"Yes! I hear you!" Joel whispered a yell.

"Where's Mia?"

"She's still sleeping. Or at least I think she's sleeping. She could be lying up there crying and in shock. I don't want to bother her until she wants to be bothered. And I don't want the cops annoying her either. I told her to text me when she gets up. That way she can tell me if she wants me to bring her breakfast, come downstairs, or just stay in her room all day."

Joel's stomach did a somersault.

"Oh my God. You know they're going to ask me if Mia told me anything. Should I tell them I knew about Dave before yesterday or do I lie?" He started to bite the remains of his thumbnail, which he'd already gnawed down to bare skin. The pain felt good. "Martin, you have to come home. You have to help me. I can't do this alone. Please, I'm begging you. Just come home before they get here so you can –"

He heard Martin sigh, then some rustling. "I'll be there in ten minutes. Hang on, Joel. Ten minutes. If I'm not home by the time the cops get there, don't answer the door."

"Okay," Joel replied. "Please hurry!"

"Don't answer the door until I'm there. Promise?"

"Yes, I promise."

"Love you," Martin snuck in before hanging up.

"Love you more," Joel answered. "Now hurry!"

Joel threw the phone onto the kitchen counter and ran upstairs. He entered the study, grabbed the binoculars he used last night from the desk and looked in the direction of Mia's house. There was one cop car, a white van void of any logo or print, and a small group of people standing behind yellow tape.

"Nosy shitheads," Joel muttered to himself.

His worry returned to the cops he'd seen walking down the street a few minutes earlier. What if they asked him if he knew about the affair Mia was having with Dave? What was he supposed to say? What answer would keep them from bringing him down to the station? His panic began to increase again and he ran down the stairs into the kitchen and grabbed the bottle of Xanax.

Did I just take one? I think I did. I can't take another one. Taking two won't kill me. Will it? No, it can't. Can it?

As his thoughts shot back and forth, the doorbell rang. Instinctively, he crouched on the floor and hid like a soldier behind the kitchen island. Martin wouldn't be home for at *least* another five or so minutes and he promised he wouldn't answer the door. But the incessant ringing and knocking were making his head spin. He *had* to answer the door. One way or the other they'd discover he was agoraphobic and never left the house; if he didn't answer now, they'd think he was hiding something.

"Man up," he whispered as he stood and wiped his hands on his shirt, as though a few swipes would remove the panic growing inside of him. "Mia is a friend, you don't know anything else. Mia is a friend, you don't know anything else. Mia is a friend, you don't know anything else."

Joel continued this chant all the way to the front door. As he opened it, the two men stood on the stoop talking to one another. Since they each wore a dress shirt and tie, Joel figured they must be higher in rank than a regular police officer.

Oh shit. Oh my God. They're detectives or sergeants or something.

When they turned toward him, the African American man offered a smile. As typically happened when someone saw him for the first time, both men's eyes locked onto his birthmark, then quickly moved to the other side of his face.

"Hi," Joel said, attempting to hide both his panic and hurt. The pain never got old. "Can I help you?" He spoke through the screen door, not courageous enough to open it and welcome in the outdoors.

The friendly-looking black man spoke first. "I'm Detective Jordan and this is Detective Halleran." He glanced behind Joel as though looking for something he'd lost. "I brought Mrs. Blythe here last night, remember?"

Joel tilted his head in an attempt to remember. The man's face didn't look familiar.

"Honestly, I don't. I think I was so worried about Mia, I didn't see or hear anything or anyone else."

"I understand," Jordan said. "How is Mrs. Blythe doing, by the way?"

"She's sleeping right now." Joel looked at Halleran, who appeared annoyed. "I helped her fall asleep around one-thirty this morning. I'm trying to let her rest as much as possible."

"And your name is Joel Peterson, is that correct?" Halleran asked, holding his pen to his pad.

"Yes. It is." He swallowed hard.

"Well, Mr. Peterson," Halleran said, "we're looking for Tom Blythe and asking neighbors if they have any idea where he might be." He paused and then, just like Detective Jordan, glanced behind him, seemingly looking for Mia. "By any chance... did Mia say anything about where she thought he might have gone?"

Joel kept his eyes on the knot of Halleran's tie, which lay about two inches beneath the opened top button of his shirt. He forced himself not to look askance, otherwise he'd see the street and panic which would force him to slam shut the door. *Where the hell is Martin?*

"No," he said, watching a droplet of sweat trickle down Halleran's temple, over his cheek and crawl beneath his jawbone. "I have no idea, and Mia's said absolutely nothing about that."

Halleran looked Joel directly in the eyes. "Did Mia ever discuss her marriage with you?"

Joel's abdomen trembled and a wave of nausea engulfed the pit of his stomach. *Martin, please hurry up.*

"Sometimes." Joel swallowed another hard gulp. "She never really went into detail about things and since it's none of my business, I didn't ask. Since I don't leave the house, she comes over every now and then to see how I'm doing."

The two detectives glanced at one another, then turned back to Joel.

"What do you mean, you 'don't leave the house?'" Jordan asked.

Just then, Martin's Porsche pulled into the driveway. Joel felt his tension slice in half. *Thank God. Martin will take care of everything.*

"Who's that?" Halleran asked, ogling the Porsche.

"That's Martin. He's my husband."

Martin shot out of the car and ran up to the stoop. He stood three steps down from the detectives. "Gentlemen, can I speak with you for a moment?"

"Martin, is it?" Halleran asked, still gawking at the sports car.

"Yes, it is."

"Well, we're in the middle of asking your... asking Joel here some questions. Once we finish up, we'd be happy to –"

Martin climbed another step. "I just need one minute, sir. Just one, please."

Joel's eyes filled with tears. This wasn't fair to Martin. He shouldn't have to go through this embarrassment just because his husband was a psycho. The ache in Joel's heart was painful, almost as much as the lump in his throat. He wanted to say something but, as was always the case, he couldn't find the courage.

The two detectives followed Martin down the steps and onto the sprawling green lawn. Joel watched the men's easily decipherable expressions as Martin explained his condition. When they turned their gazes from Martin to Joel, he knew his husband must've told them that he hadn't left the house for years. Their faces showed the question most people would ask – *Why would someone want to live a life like that?* It was a question Joel asked himself at least ten times a day.

They continued to listen politely as Martin talked. Halleran scribbled into his notepad and Jordan played footsie with the blades of fresh fescue. Within three minutes, Martin was shaking both their hands and nodding them away. They walked toward the Porsche, where they stopped to take a closer look, before finally leaving.

As Martin sauntered up the steps toward the front door, Joel heard Halleran mumble to Jordan: "This is one nutty neighborhood."

Joel smiled. *He has no idea.*

Martin grabbed the screen door handle, pulled it, came inside and kissed Joel on the cheek. "Let's go inside," he whispered, closing the door behind him.

Martin took Joel's hand and led him to the living room sofa. The simple touch of his fingers gave Joel a sense of calm he hadn't felt in hours. Although he was still trembling and felt weak and sweaty, having Martin by his side was like taking a Valium or Xanax. Even better. The man quieted his thoughts and eased his anxieties in ways that no prescription drug could.

"What happened?" he asked. "What did you tell them?"

Sitting side by side, Martin placed his hand over Joel's. "I had to be honest. I told them about your agoraphobia and your anxieties. I told them you wouldn't have seen anything because the blinds are usually closed. And you wouldn't have heard anything because we're so far away from Mia's house. Long story short, they said if they feel they need more info from you, one of them will come by and talk with you inside the house so you don't have to go outside."

Joel laid his head on Martin's shoulder, a sense of relief washing over him like the smoothest of surfer waves. "I don't know why you put up with me. I really don't."

Martin stroked Joel's face. "Because I love you. No other reason, babe. No other reason." He pushed Joel's hair back behind his ears and kissed his birthmark from the top of the boot to the tip of its heel. "By the way, I'm proud that you were brave enough to answer the door and speak to them. Maybe the Paxil is helping. Fingers crossed."

Paxil, Shmaxil, Joel thought. *I lost my mind for a few seconds. That's why I answered the door. I had no idea what I was doing.*

"Did they say anything else about Tom?" he asked, rubbing Martin's crossed fingers.

"No. Just that they're looking for him and trying to find any possible lead."

"Mia and I were up half the night trying to figure out how Tom found out about Dave. He *never* came home in the middle of the day, but for some reason he showed up yesterday with a gun in his hand and walked right into the bedroom. No one knew about Dave except for me... at least that's what Mia told me."

Joel tightened his grip on Martin's hand. "Did they ask you if *you* knew about Dave? That I told you what was going on between them?"

Martin shook his head.

"What if they come back and ask if I knew about Dave? I can't lie. If I lie, they'll find out I lied. If I don't lie, they'll think I covered things up or even that I told Tom about it. What if they want to question me down at the precinct or station or whatever they call it? I can't go there. If they make me –"

Martin rose and stood in front of Joel, placing his hands on his shoulders so he wouldn't start pacing again.

"No matter what, you'll tell the truth. It always comes out in the end anyway. You were Mia's only confidant and that's the truth. There's no reason anyone would think you're guilty of anything except being a good friend. You have absolutely nothing to worry about. I promise." He looked around the room. "Where's your phone?"

"Kitchen island, I think."

Joel watched Martin get his phone, pour a Xanax from the vial into his hand and grab a Poland Spring from the fridge on the way back into the living room. He handed Joel the pill and water and then placed his cellphone on the end table.

"Take the Xanax and lie down on the sofa," Martin instructed. Joel obeyed without argument and without disclosing that he'd just taken one before the detectives arrived. "I want you to rest while I go back to work. I'll call you later to check up on you."

Joel rested his head on the sofa cushion and swung his legs onto the couch. He took a deep breath.

"What about Mia?" he asked.

"I have a feeling she'll be sleeping for quite a while. Plus you told her to text you if she needs you, right?" Joel nodded sluggishly. "Remember, I'm supposed to have that client dinner-slash-meeting tonight. Would you rather I cancel?"

Joel closed his eyes and shook his head.

"No, no," he stammered. "Please don't cancel. If we need you, we'll call you." His voice was fading.

Martin kissed Joel's forehead. "Your phone is on the table. It's just a few inches away."

Joel smiled and puckered his lips as though Martin was standing above him about to kiss him goodbye. When he heard the front door close, he realized Martin was gone and unpursed his mouth.

With his eyes closed, he searched the table beside the sofa for his phone. When he found it, he put it on his chest and took a deep breath.

"I'm here, Mia," he mumbled. "I'm just a few inches away."

Within seconds, Joel had fallen asleep, prepared to pass from one nightmare into another.

CHAPTER 6

It took Scott almost an hour after Jordan and Halleran left before he found the courage to sit at his desk and open the laptop.

The fear about his responsibility for what happened to Mr. Hedge Fund gripped him by the throat. Would they somehow find out he was behind the whole thing and throw him in jail for the rest of his life? But how could they? He'd taken every precaution. Besides, they were looking for Tom, who they already *knew* was the killer. There was no way it could come back to him... unless...

"Shut up already!" *You finally have something to work with and you're squandering it on senseless worry. You have an extramarital affair, a jealous husband, a murder and a police investigation. And that's just the start!*

"It doesn't get much better than that," he said aloud. "Now get to work, for Christ's sake."

Two hours later he was still staring at a white screen. Scott rumbled with frustration as the screen stared back – tormenting him, making a mockery out of what he'd done to Mia and Tom. Was it all for nothing? The page was *still* blank. His fingers sat on the keys, waiting, hoping, biding their time for the first wave of words to spill out like a midsummer monsoon. But he had nothing.

"You need more" he said to himself.

Yeah, that's it. What went down yesterday wasn't going to be enough. He needed more action, additional flawed characters. Sure, infidelity and crimes of passion were a great enticement for his readers, but they were a bit trite. It was critical for him to develop another character or two who added intrigue and mystery to the Mia and Tom situation. Someone with strange traits and shortcomings, maybe even physical defects. Someone exactly like...

Joel Peterson.

By now the police were probably blocks away, so he'd be able to make an unplanned visit to Joel's without running into the law. He'd start the conversation with what had happened at the Blythe's and then try to delve further into Joel's persona. Was it a specific trauma that kept him hidden in the house? What did he enjoy doing? What did he hate doing? What was his *real* relationship with Martin? Did he have any friends? Was all his communication with the outside world via the Internet?

He had so many questions for Joel, he could barely wait to get out the door. He grabbed his cellphone and keys and rushed onto the porch, down the path and onto the sidewalk. As he strolled, he smirked, the opportunity of getting new details about one of his main characters getting more real with each step he took.

The sun was beginning to set and the yellowish glow of incandescent bulbs fell onto his neighbors' front lawns. He could see movement within a few of the homes, but wouldn't dare look for too long. He didn't want to be like most of the locals in the community, gawkers who were always peeking into his windows from afar. He'd offer a wave, mostly for the sake of book sales, but when he'd catch them gazing at his house or driving by slowly to show their friends where Scott Atwood lived, it took every ounce of energy he had not to turn his wave into a middle-finger salute.

As he neared Joel's house, he noticed a black, unmarked car parked in front. With daylight fading fast, he couldn't make out any details other than two male figures sitting inside. The driver sipped from a water bottle as the passenger poured the remaining coffee from a thermos out his window and into the street. Scott attempted to ignore them and stroll up Joel's walkway when the man in the passenger seat opened the car door.

"Hold up," the man said.

Scott halted and turned toward the voice. The man looked him up and down as he made his way over, stopping only when his face was inches away from Scott's. He couldn't have been more than twenty-six years old but had the demeanor of a veteran cop at least three decades on the force.

"Yes?" Scott replied, still unsure who this child officer was and why he wasn't allowing Scott to walk up to Joel's front door.

"What's your name?"

"Scott Atwood." Scott pointed toward his house. "I live three houses down."

The young man looked down the block then back to Scott, gazing directly into his eyes.

"Did Mr. Peterson invite you here?"

With that question, it became obvious to Scott that these were two undercover cops recruited to either protect a very paranoid agoraphobic or... could Mia be inside Joel's house? He knew Joel and Mia were friendly, but were they close enough for her to run to him in time of crisis? This could be his chance to kill two birds with one stone – get all the information he needed about his two main characters with one visit. It would be the timesaver he needed to get his book underway and Grace off his back.

"No, but we're friends. I'm Scott Atwood."

"Yeah, I heard you the first time," the young cop responded.

"Does the name sound familiar to you?"

"No, should it?" he quipped.

Scott rolled his eyes. It would surprise him if this kid could read a license plate let alone a novel.

"Can I see Joel, please?"

"Hold on." He turned toward the unmarked car. "Jackie!" he yelled. "Check with Mr. Peterson on a Scott Atwood."

Scott heard a voice emerge from somewhere in the near darkness. "Got it," it said.

The officer continued to glare at him and as Scott's anxiety started to peak, the young cop asked, "So you famous or something?"

Scott let out a subtle sigh. "I'm an author."

"Huh. Whattaya write?"

"Books," Scott joked, trying to keep the officer on his good side. By the cop's expression, it didn't work. "I'm kidding. Did you ever hear of the novels, 'Don't Be Fooled' or 'Dying to Tell?'"

The childlike cop shook his head.

"I don't do much reading. But when I do, it's usually about zombies and shit like that."

Holy shit. I have a real genius on my hands. C'mon Jackie. Give me the go-ahead for Christ's sake.

Scott tried to keep the conversation going the best he could. He had to find a way to get inside and talk to Joel and possibly Mia. He was too close to learning about his characters to give up now.

"Well there are a lot of good post-apocalyptic novels out there today. I've even read a few myself." *Yeah, right.* "Usually during plane trips when I..."

"Hey Sam, Mr. P. says he's good to go."

Thank God. Scott almost said the words aloud; he couldn't get away from this guy fast enough.

"You're good to go," Sam said slowly turning and walking back toward the car. "Maybe I'll get one of your books."

Scott headed up the walkway and waved.

"If you do, come by and I'll sign it for you!" he yelled to the officer, but the cop was already in the car, oblivious to Scott's offer as he scrambled through a box of stale donuts.

When he reached the front door he was about to ring the bell when he remembered Joel once admitting that loud noises scared him. While he was at it, he'd also confessed that he was petrified of lightning and the smell of smoke. *No cozy nights by the fire with Martin, that's for sure.* So to start off on Joel's good side, Scott tapped lightly on the glass slats of the jalousie entry door.

Joel opened the large wooden door behind it and squinted through the louvers. "Scott?" he asked, cross-eyed and looking as though he'd just awoken from six months of hibernation.

"The one and only. How you doin', Joel?"

Joel combed his fingers through his hair. "I'm okay," he replied, his partially opened eyes darting behind Scott to make sure the unmarked car was still there. "Sort of just woke up from a nap when I got the call you were here. How are you?"

"I'm good, thanks. Should I come back... is there a better time for me to..." Scott stammered. He'd expected to be invited in by now and this unanticipated lack of hospitality left him speechless. After a few more seconds, he broke the uncomfortable silence. "I heard what happened yesterday. What a shame. A real tragedy."

"Yeah," Joel said, his hands now in the front pockets of his jeans.

"I just thought as neighbors... well, maybe we could just hang out for a little while." Scott paused when Joel turned his head and glanced toward the staircase. When he turned back around, his face was wrapped in an expression of distress. There was now no doubt that Mia was somewhere in the house. "Honestly, I was feeling a little lonely... I mean with everything that happened... I just... well..."

Joel's expression softened. "Come in," he said, gesturing for Scott to open the jalousie door himself. He leaned closer to the door and whispered, "But you should know that Mia is here."

Scott stopped mid-step.

"I figured as much when they basically had to announce my arrival" he whispered back, the trembling of excitement again revving its engine in his gut. "I didn't know you two were friends."

Joel rubbed his birthmark and pinched the inside corners of his bloodshot eyes with the tip of his thumb and forefinger. "Yes. We're friends. She's upstairs sleeping, so we have to be quiet. I want her to rest."

"I understand. But why does she need protection?" Scott asked.

"They haven't found Tom yet. They want to protect her in case he shows up."

Scott had a million questions but didn't want to ask another until he was behind closed doors and gave Joel a chance to get comfortable with his presence. He stepped carefully inside and didn't move until Joel closed the door behind him and led him into the living room. Joel grabbed each pillow on the loveseat one by one and puffed them up. After about a minute or so, he examined his work and finally asked Scott to sit down.

"Johnny Walker Black, no ice?"

"Wow, how did you remember that?" Scott looked around the room, noticing how everything was in its place. *Agoraphobic. Paranoid. Anxious* and *OCD. This poor son of a –*

"The senate race event Martin and I hosted here. I could tell you didn't really like the wine, even though you were drinking it. I asked you what your favorite drink was. You said, 'Johnny Walker Black, no ice.'"

This guy has got to be part of my story.

"Well, you have a great memory." He looked at his watch. "I'd love one, but it's only twelve o'clock in the afternoon."

"And your point?"

Oh my God, is that a sense of humor?

"You're right. It's been a long day and it's only lunchtime. I'll take you up on the offer."

After handing Scott a half-filled crystal scotch glass, Joel sat down in the Cavendar wingback chair across from Scott.

"Nothing for you?"

"No. Not yet." Joel forced a smile.

By the dazed look on his face, it was obvious some kind of drug was already in his system trying its hardest to keep him calm. He held the tumbler up as if to clink Joel's invisible glass.

"To Mia," Scott whispered.

"To Mia," Joel responded, his eyes once again passing a glance at the staircase.

The scotch warmed its way down Scott's throat and within a few seconds he could feel his body begin to unwind. Joel was more relaxed than when he'd first arrived, but he was still tight-lipped. From his demeanor and lack of mental clarity, Scott quickly realized he'd have to initiate any potential conversation. It was obvious Joel wasn't about to give up anything by his own free will, so he took another sip and cleared his throat.

"I'm worried about Mia," he said. Joel's eyes widened. Scott's hope of getting a reaction was met with success, so he continued without pause. "The cops said she's okay physically, but, if I remember correctly, they said, 'mentally she's under a lot of stress.'"

Scott took a sip of scotch and let his words sit. Joel turned toward the dining room, then back to the kitchen, then to the hallway behind Scott that led to the great room. He was doing everything he could not to look directly at him.

"How *is* she doing?" He looked away from Joel, hoping the lack of eye contact would help loosen Joel's lips. His gaze fell upon a photo of Joel and Martin sitting on their back deck, the creek behind them, clinking champagne flutes as though celebrating something – perhaps the fact that Joel was outside. *Jesus, what a poor, sad nutjob.*

"The best she can," he mumbled. "She's doing the best she can."

"To be honest, I can only think of one situation that would bring about something like this."

Joel didn't say a word.

"I can only assume" – Scott tried to choose his words carefully – "that Mia was seeing someone and Tom found out. He came home, caught them together and shot the guy."

Joel remained silent.

"I mean, we know Mia and Tom never really had the best marriage. And we *also* know that Tom has anger issues. So... is that what happened?"

Joel glanced out the massive windows overlooking the backyard. Scott could almost see the words on the tip of his tongue, but the man held back, still unable to utter the answer.

"Joel..." Scott muted his voice a bit. "I don't mean to be nosy, but it's going to come out anyway. Every local TV station is covering it, not to mention all the local online tabloids. The details will be leaked bit by bit to the press, and by tomorrow Mia's personal life will be public domain. So you really don't need to worry about telling me anything."

Joel glared at Scott. "Why are you asking me these questions? Why did you come here? Are you looking for information for the cops or something?"

Scott took another sip of scotch and leaned back into the loveseat. He had to play this right, otherwise his plan to get intel about his main characters would be dead in the water.

"Honestly, I like Mia," he said. Joel looked at him and tilted his head. "Every time I've met or spoken with her, she's seemed like a wonderful woman. If what I said is true, and she *was* with someone else yesterday, I wouldn't think any less of her. Now that I know how close the two of you are, I want you to know that I have a lot of contacts who could possibly help her with... well, with problems that might arise from what happened." Scott inched forward. "Basically, I'm here to help."

He left his words hanging in midair and took another sip of scotch.

After about a minute of outlining his birthmark with his index finger, Joel fell back into his chair and let out a huge sigh. Scott watched him listen intently to the silence, obviously trying to make sure Mia wasn't up and about.

"Dave. His name was Dave. She loved him. He loved her. It's been going on for about a year." Joel's expression changed from that of a man in anguish to someone who just let the world roll off his shoulders. "I'm sure she's going to need help in some way. And I'm even more certain she'd appreciate anything you could do for her. I can help from an emotional perspective, but I don't have the kind of contacts that you probably do." He started rubbing his birthmark again.

Before Scott had a chance to respond, Joel's phone beeped.

"It's Mia," he said while texting with his thumbs faster than anything Scott had ever witnessed. "I told her to text me when she got up."

Scott leaned forward. *Holy shit. I might actually get to meet another one of my main characters! Talk about luck!*

Still texting, Joel said, "She's going to take a shower and get herself together. She said she'll come downstairs in about fifteen minutes. I'm not sure you should be here when she does."

Pretending he didn't hear a word the man said, Scott swallowed the remaining scotch and watched as Joel walked to the windows overlooking the front yard. He slid the phone into the back pocket of his jeans and opened up the café-style shutters.

"Did she say how she's doing?" Scott asked.

There was silence. Joel appeared to be looking up and down the street.

"Is she okay?" Scott asked louder, trying to regain Joel's attention. It was as though he'd forgotten he had a guest. *Are dissociative episodes also part of his issues, or has he still not woken up from his Xanax-induced coma?*

Joel continued to gaze out the window. "She didn't say. I know it's weird since we were only texting, but her words sound tired."

Scott was about to inquire further into her texts when Joel let out a soft giggle.

"There goes Brad. There's a murder right around the corner from him and he still goes jogging away in his preppy Harvard sweatshirt," he stated out of the blue. "Now *there's* a story."

Scott stood straight up like a soldier when a commander enters the room. *Who's this Brad and what kind of story does he have?*

"What do you mean?" he asked nonchalantly.

Joel swiped his middle finger along the top of the shutters, looking for dust. "Nothing. I didn't mean anything by it."

Scott wasn't buying it. Anyone who says, "now *there's* a story" knows there's a story. He just had to find out what it was before he got kicked out.

"Spill it, Joel. Tell me about Mr. Harvard. I'll keep it between us, I promise."

Joel kept his gaze toward the street without moving a muscle. Scott followed his stare and caught a glimpse of a young kid he'd seen jogging the neighborhood just about every day.

"Brad Sheehan is extremely hot," Joel said, unembarrassed by his own admission. "Remember that Christmas party Martin made me give last year? Ugh."

"Yes," Scott replied, not as surprised by that fact that Joel let it be known he didn't want the party, but more by the fact that it still bothered him.

"Well, his parents had him drop off the bottle of Caymus Cab they forgot to bring. When he showed up at the door, I almost fell over. *Gorgeous* in every way. Straight black hair – black as coal. His eyes are literally emerald green, I mean, they literally shine a deep green like I've never seen before. And his face is perfect in every way. He's like a male model going to one of the best colleges in the country. And he's going to be a doctor."

"Better watch out before I tell Martin," Scott joked.

"Oh, please. I told Martin about Brad the second he ran off after handing me the wine."

Scott rolled his eyes. "So that's the story? A hot guy is going to med school?"

Joel didn't respond.

Goddamnit. This is like pulling teeth.

"Joel," Scott repeated, "*that's* the story about Brad?"

"Well, he's a coke addict," Joel said, so matter of fact, Scott had to hold back laughter. "At least, I *think* it's cocaine. He's addicted to other drugs, too. I'm just not sure what they are."

"And you know this *how*?"

Joel hesitated then let out a deep sigh. Scott could tell his questions were irritating Joel, but he didn't care. The subplots for his book were hanging in the balance. "Well, at the party, his parents were talking about how perfect Brad is. How proud they are of him and all the wonderful things he's going to do. They said he was home for the holidays and was spending a lot of time in his room doing extra work so he could stay ahead in his classes. I was in the room upstairs one night looking for some file or something. I can't remember. When I looked out the window, I saw Brad's light on and saw him snorting coke, at least I think it was coke, all by himself."

Jesus, Scott thought, *this guy is a trove of information. This Brad has to be another character in the book.*

"I wouldn't call someone who snorts coke one time an addict," Scott said. "Maybe it was just an isolated case, a way for him to stay up and study."

Joel turned around and headed toward the kitchen. "No, he's done it more than once. Pretty much every time he's home for break he's putting something up his nose or popping some kind of pill."

"Christ, that sucks. There's going to be a drug addict taking care of sick people one day?" *Hmmm, that could be a great part of the plot.*

"Yeah, I know. Crazy, right?"

"What's crazy is the fact that you know so much about a kid that lives across the creek. I mean it's not *that* far, but still, you have to have pretty good eyesight to see into his room." Scott faked a laugh. "I mean seriously, can you see that well or do you use a telescope?"

Joel picked at his birthmark, his eyes locked on the Xanax bottle sitting on the kitchen counter. "I can see that well."

Scott hid a smile. *An* eagle *can't see that well.*

As soon as they heard the sound of footsteps heading toward them, they turned their heads in unison.

"Shit," Joel whispered before he started to rush down the hallway to meet her. "She's not going to want you here."

Scott followed and stopped at least ten feet behind him, taking in the scene.

Mia didn't seem to see him, her eyes fixed on Joel. Before she even reached his outstretched arms, she started to sob. Joel held her head to his chest and kissed her forehead.

"Shhh..." he said quietly. "Shhh... it'll be okay. Everything will be okay."

Scott watched both of them in disbelief. Up until this moment he'd been able to rationalize what he'd done, but there was something about this beautiful, innocent woman that made his stomach turn. The burn from the scotch worked its way back into his throat and he pushed it down, along with his remorse, by swallowing hard.

He suddenly had this dreadful feeling he'd be doing a lot of that in the weeks to come.

***

Almost five minutes had passed before Joel could settle Mia down enough to bring her into the living room. He gently sat her by his side on the sofa, across from the loveseat on which Scott had been seated a few seconds earlier. After sitting in silence for what seemed an eternity, he cleared his throat.

As quick as a flash, her expression changed from anguish to confusion to something resembling anger.

"Why is he..." Mia started, her voice still quivering.

Joel put his arm around her shoulder and held her tightly. He gave Scott an annoyed look and half-shrugged his shoulders. "He's here to help."

She stared at Scott without uttering another sound.

Is it possible? Does she have any idea I caused this? How could she...

"Maybe I should leave," Scott said. The scotch burned his throat again as he stood. "I could come back tomorrow or maybe..."

"No. Sit down, please," Joel said. He stroked Mia's hair. "Mia, Scott's here because he wants to help. Between the cops scouring the neighborhood and the news people vomiting their gossip, we're going to need some help now – and probably more after this is no longer front-page news." He kissed the top of her head. "Scott has a lot of contacts and knows people who can help with a lot of the crap that will need to be taken care of. He's here to help."

Mia raised her head to look at Joel.

"Does he know... about... Dave?"

Whew! Scott's entire body released its tension like a broken dam. *Thank God. She doesn't know that I know.*

"Yes," Joel replied somberly. She buried her face in the crook of his neck and started to weep. "Shhh... it's okay. It's okay."

Scott wanted nothing more than to go home and write while Mia's emotions were fresh on his mind. Her sadness and grief were so tangible, they reached deep inside of him and although he knew he should feel sorrow for her, he felt jubilance instead. Feeling her emotions was a breath of fresh air; her pain was helping to dissolve his writer's block and he needed to get to his laptop before the emotions escaped.

But he couldn't leave. He had to get her to trust him enough to disclose more about her life and maybe, even, the love she just lost. He also feared that leaving might raise suspicion. But then he began to wonder if staying might do the same.

You're being paranoid.

He sat back down on the loveseat. Mia turned her face from the crook of Joel's neck to look at him, her wet eyes unblinking.

"Mia," Scott said softly. "I'm not judging anyone. I'm not asking any questions. I'm not offering any advice. Like Joel said, I'm just here to help." She kept her eyes on his without saying a word. "I've had to do a lot of research for my books and I know some of the..." *Don't say 'gory.' Don't say 'grisly.'* "Some of the details that need attending to. Those are just some of the things I can help with."

Mia's eyelids were scarlet, almost ruby red from what must've been hours of crying. Her eyes, however, shone a turquoise blue, like the crystal clear waters of Aruba. Even with tracks of mascara running down her cheeks, random sprouts in her pulled-back hair and a wrinkled, oversized shirt that made her appear half her true size, her beauty was unmistakable. It was immediately apparent to

Scott why Mr. Hedge Fund found a way to see this woman every week. Her beauty was almost overwhelming, and as she stared into his eyes, breathing became an effort for him.

Mia didn't respond to his offer of help. She just looked at Scott as though she'd lost her sense of hearing.

"Is that okay, Mia?" Joel asked, his mark of Italy leaning against the top of her head.

She nodded. "Yes," she said, barely audible.

Scott unintentionally nodded in rhythm with hers. Then it hit him, like a smack across the face.

Jesus Christ. Mia is the protagonist of my story. She's the protagonist, the 'good' lead character who must survive, who finds her way through hell and rises from the ashes to a victorious outcome. And that makes me exactly who my character should be – the antagonist! The piece of shit who causes her pain and then fights her every step of the way to ensure she fails in the end. And if this is going to be a psychological thriller, then, holy shit, I have to start playing mind games.

He looked into her eyes and their pain shot through him like an arrow striking his chest. From out of nowhere the ache in his right arm returned. Not wanting to make a scene, he jumped up and started walking to the door when he heard Mia say something to him. He grabbed his arm and turned around.

"I'm sorry," he mumbled. "Did you say something?"

Both Joel and Mia glanced up at him, their heads tipping in unison.

"No," Mia said.

"Where are you going?" Joel asked. "We have to talk about..."

"Let Mia rest now," Scott interrupted. "I'll come back tomorrow and we can talk about what needs to be done."

The ache in his arm was now throbbing and an odd sound of muffled voices grew loud in his head. It was impossible to decipher any words but the noise made him feel as though he were in the midst of a crowd at a baseball game where the chatter was just an unintelligible chorus of sound.

"Joel, I'll call you in the morning. Mia..." He felt a lump in his throat as she looked up at him with a mixed expression of sorrow and desperation. "You get some rest, if you can. I'll be back tomorrow."

As Scott walked toward the front door, he heard Joel's voice. "*He doesn't look good.*" Scott spun around, focusing his gaze on Joel.

"What?" Scott asked.

With his head still leaning against Mia's, Joel turned to Scott. "What do you mean, 'what?'"

"Didn't you just say..." Scott started. "I could've sworn you just said, 'he doesn't look good.'"

"To be honest, I *was* thinking that, but I didn't say it out loud. Are you a mind reader now?"

"Yeah," Scott swung around and headed back toward the front door. "I'm a mind reader."

Once he closed the door behind him, he sat on the top step. With his palms pressing against his closed eyes, he rested his head and tried to ignore the pain in his arm and the nonsensical voices in his head.

Yeah, Joel. I'm a mind reader. A mind reader who's losing his mind.

CHAPTER 7

Brad pulled off his Harvard sweatshirt and studied his body in the large, pivoting floor mirror that stood in the corner of his bedroom.

Running his index finger along the indentation of his perspiration-filled six-pack, he shook his head with approval. He could almost feel the striation of muscle beneath his finger and the results of his run were making the ordeal of this morning worth it. Today's jog was tougher than usual. Between the extreme humidity and trying to avoid the cop cars, spectators and gossiping neighbors lining the sidewalks, his run felt more like an obstacle course than a jog. And to make matters worse, he'd been forced to wear a knit sweatshirt through the entire exercise.

An hour before, on his way out of the house to run, his father stopped him in the living room. He tugged at the strap of Brad's netted tank top.

"What's this? Shouldn't you be wearing your Harvard sweatshirt?"

"Dad, it's like ninety degrees out there and ninety-eight percent humidity. I'll collapse if I wear that sweatshirt."

His father rolled his eyes. "First of all, Bradley, take the skirt off. You won't collapse. Your body will work harder and you'll lose some of that body fat that refuses to come off." He tried to pinch Brad's taut stomach but Brad pulled away before he had the chance. "Secondly, you want people to know that you're a Harvard student. Show it off. Tell the world. It's costing us enough!"

His father laughed as he softly slapped Brad's cheek. Brad smiled back, despite wanting to punch the man as hard as he could in his solar plexus. He was used to that desire, feeling it every second of most days. It was about the tenth time this week his father had mentioned the cost of sending him to Harvard. Jesus. The man had millions. Like a few hundred thousand was going to deprive him of his quarterly excursions to Oahu and Bora Bora. Brad's schooling was a drop in the bucket and yet his father couldn't help but make it sound as though he didn't know where their next meal was coming from.

"How about I get a few Harvard tanks for running?" he asked, almost out the door.

"That's fine," his father responded, leaning back in the leather recliner and snapping the pages of his Wall Street Journal. "But today, wear the sweatshirt."

His tone spoke volumes. Brad knew he had no choice. He ran up the stairs to his room to change his shirt, silently cursing every step of the way.

Now, back from his run and still sweating profusely, Brad grabbed the towel from the hook on the back of the door and wiped himself down. The cell phone on his desk was buzzing, but he ignored it. It was most likely one of his friends wanting to hit a party or club. That would be impossible. His father had coerced his longtime friend Dr. Mendham at Yale New Haven Hospital to let Brad intern a few days a week. Tomorrow was one of those days. He had to be in New Haven by 6:00 AM to waste his day reviewing paperwork with patients, filing x-rays and doing whatever other inane tasks were asked of him. His father never even told him he'd set up this internship. He and Mendham had decided amongst themselves how and where Brad would spend his summer. As was typically the case, Brad had no choice in the matter.

"Idle hands are the devil's workshop," his father had said since the day Brad was old enough to understand language. And he made sure to repeat it during every phone call they'd had before summer break began. It was his father's way of making sure Brad understood one significant fact: time off from school didn't mean time off from moving his career forward.

But the buzzing phone was insistent. *Maybe, if I tell one of them I'm not going out, they'll spread the word and everyone will stop texting me.* So he grabbed the phone. When he saw the contact's name and photo, he fell back against the wall.

hey, Felicia had texted. Her profile pic hadn't changed. His heart sank.

hey, he texted back, keeping an eye on the bedroom door.

miss u

miss u 2

Can I see u?

When? He walked to the door and leaned against it.

Now? :)

Can't. Yale work tomorrow.

Friday?

Yes. After internship hours. 4:00. Front of 40 York.

2 days? Really?

I'm sorry. Wish it could be sooner.

I'll b there.

I luv u.

<3. Luv u 2.

He tossed the phone onto the unmade bed.

Walking to the window, Brad stared straight ahead, through the thin branches of the oak tree that reached his third-floor window. Though the leaves blocked some of his view, he could still see a few people paddling their inflatable rafts down the creek, as well as some lights from the homes on the other side of the water.

He swallowed hard against the lump in his throat. It had been three months since the abortion and he hadn't seen Felicia since the day he'd gone with her to the procedure. Afterward they'd driven in silence until reaching her house.

"Please don't call me," she begged, her voice quivering. "I'll be in touch when I'm ready." She looked deep into his eyes, the tears streaming down her cheeks. "Promise, me, Brad. Promise me."

"I promise," he mouthed, unable to speak.

She ran out of the car and was inside the house within seconds. His voice coming back in a rush, but too late, he'd yelled after her but there was no response. It took almost five minutes before he stopped crying and could see clearly enough to step on the gas pedal and drive away.

The abortion was something he and Felicia had discussed incessantly for weeks, neither able to make up their minds, and each pushing aside the fact that every day they did nothing was a day closer to having the decision made for them. They knew they were too young to have a child, that there was too much ahead of them to prepare for without a baby taking up every second of their day. Felicia had just started her art career and Brad was spending every waking hour studying for his medical exams. The truth was simple: there was no possible way for them to be able to take care of a child. Yet they'd continually talk through it as though somehow an alternative exit out of a circular maze would magically appear.

But it didn't and the inevitable decision hung in limbo until one night after they'd hung up from a two-hour conversation and Brad's bedroom door opened. His father walked in without saying a word and sat in the chair beside the desk. Brad was lying on his bed, feet up on the wall above the headboard, staring at the ceiling with his phone on his bare chest.

"Get rid of it," his father said, obviously having eavesdropped on their conversation. "It's for your own good."

Brad, unable to respond, kept his gaze on the spotless white ceiling. Had he listened in on all their calls, or was this the only one? Was he listening at the door while they'd had sex in this bedroom? Were there cameras? Microphones? Was any of his life private anymore?

"Put an end to this now," his father said, "and you'll be a prominent doctor with a great career. Get tied down with a wife and a kid and you can kiss your future, *and my money,* goodbye."

With that, he slowly stood, walked out the door and gently closed it behind him.

Brad wanted to run after him and start screaming: You selfish piece of shit! All you think about is money and status! What about me? What about my *feelings?* What about what Felicia is going through? What is *wrong* with you? You're a son of a bitch narcissist shithole who only thinks about himself! I hate you!

But Brad didn't run after him and didn't utter a word. He knew it would only be a waste of breath and make the entire situation a whole lot worse. About to jump out of his skin, his body ached for something, anything, to forget his circumstances and pretend that what was happening, wasn't.

He glanced at the closet door, then quickly turned away in shame. Although somewhere deep down he knew that he'd eventually snort the cocaine hidden inside the sneaker box at the back of his closet, the act of pretending for just a few seconds gave him a sense of hope. But, as was always the case, at the end of that hope came surrender to one of his few weaknesses. So after carefully checking the hallway to make certain his father was nowhere nearby, he opened the closet door and released a sigh that could only be compared to a death rattle.

The following evening at dinner, not one word was uttered until the awkward silence started to suffocate Brad. He inhaled deeply and as he let it out, he started to speak, unsure of what he was going to say.

"Dad, please. Listen..."

"No discussion here, Brad. You need to put an end to this... this... debacle and then stop seeing her. She's only after your money anyway. *My* money, I should say. So it's best if you cut her out of your life, at least until you're a resident. By that time, you'll be well on your way to where you need to be. You'll probably have forgotten about her by then anyway."

Brad looked to his mother sitting in the seat across from him. Through the arrangement of tulips and dahlias placed on the table moments before by their housekeeper Suelen, he could only see her eyes staring back, accompanied by her typical expression of impotence.

Brad felt betrayed... again. He knew she wouldn't say a word, wouldn't have an opinion, wouldn't cause conflict with the man who ran her world. Brad begged her with his eyes to say something, anything that might help him convince this soulless fool that he loved Felicia and they might be able to figure out a way to have a family *and* stay on course at Harvard. But his mother simply used her fork to fiddle with her basmati rice, pretending to search her plate for something she'd never find.

There was no arguing. And Brad knew it. Trying to get the man to understand anything that involved feelings or emotions was like spitting into the wind. The most depressing thing was that he knew his father was right about the baby. Having a child would devastate their lives and put an end to both their dreams before they even got started. Both he and Felicia knew it, however it was his father's callousness and indifference to saying it out loud that made him realize ending the pregnancy was the only way out.

He threw his napkin onto the plate still loaded with food and stood.

"I'm done," he said running toward the stairs to his bedroom. "Done!"

It was almost 11:00 PM when he snuck Felicia inside the house and up to his room. After talking, crying and cuddling together all night, they'd made their decision only minutes before the sun rose over the creek behind the house: they'd go to the clinic together today and end the pregnancy before the weekend.

He waited for his father to leave for work before sneaking Felicia out of the house and to her car parked at the end of the block. When they reached it, he opened the door, kissed her gently on the lips and hugged her as though it was the last moment they'd ever spend together.

"Are you sure?" he whispered in her ear. "Did we make the right decision?"

When she looked in his eyes, tears teetered on the rims of her lids. "Yes," she said, although her voice was quivering. "I'll make the arrangements and call you with the details."

"I love you," he whispered.

"I love you."

He watched her drive away and walked barefoot back to the house, heartbroken over their choice but taking solace in the fact that although his father had insisted they end the pregnancy, it was he and Felicia who made the final decision together.

And he thought they'd made the right one... until tonight – their first contact in three months. He hadn't realized until this very moment how much he missed her silky skin, her lips, the feel of her naked body against his.

He had acquiesced to her request not to call her, but it was more difficult than he thought. At first he'd dial her number and hang up before it started to ring. He didn't want to break his promise, but not being able to hear her voice had become both mentally and physically painful. After a week, he figured out ways to help ease the pain – more cocaine to help keep his thoughts at bay, an extra dose or two of Xanax to help him sleep at night. Sometimes he'd resort to snorting some of the oxycodone he'd saved from his ankle injury a year earlier. He buried himself in class assignments and course reading. Anything to keep his mind busy or blank. But there was a problem. Once the drugs wore off or he had a lull in school work, the pain would return and often feel worse than when he'd first made the promise. It was a vicious cycle, a rollercoaster that never stopped twisting and turning. The worst part was that he knew what was happening to him, had read about it in many a textbook, but he found it impossible to get off the ride.

Brad paced his bedroom in anticipation. Of what, he wasn't sure, but his insides trembled and his mind raced uncontrollably. He blamed his father. For the hollowness the man constantly dug into the pit of his only son's stomach... for the way he kept his wife's mouth closed with just a glance... for how he used money and power to force others to take action they abhorred.

His mind reeled back to the day he turned 8 years old. The birthday cake that had been tailor-made for his party was monstrous, a delectable dessert built with layers of vanilla buttercream that also covered the entire surface. Still, it was too large for ten children to finish so there was plenty left over when everyone had gone home, leaving Brad at the kitchen island watching Suelen clean up the mess the kids had made.

"I want more cake," he said with a whimper. "It's my birthday. I want more cake."

It was then he felt the warmth of bony fingers on his shoulder. A jolt ran through him and he shuddered, knowing there was only one person who could scare him without uttering a word. Brad didn't move... he just waited.

Finally, the voice spoke. "We discussed this already," his father said. "The more cake you eat, the fatter you get. Is that what you want? Do you want to be fat?"

Brad peered down at the island, tracing the quartz's veiny line with his finger. He shook his head.

"Then why do you keep asking for cake?"

His father didn't sound overly upset this time, so he thought he might have a chance. He slowly turned the stool around where his eyes met his father's chest.

"It's my birthday. I should be able to each as much cake as I want."

Silence.

"It's my birthday," Brad repeated, softer this time, a whine that hung on the verge of crying. "Why can't I eat my cake?"

His father let out a sigh. "Suelen, stop cleaning. Take the rest of the cake from the refrigerator, place it on the counter in front of Brad and please provide a fork."

"Yes, Mr. Sheehan," Suelen replied, her feet moving so quickly they reminded Brad of a card deck being shuffled.

In less than a minute, half of the enormous cake sat on its glass platter in front of Brad, a fork and napkin along its side. His father sat down on the stool beside him, leaned back and glared at him. At that moment, Brad's desire for cake disappeared. His anxiety worked its way throughout his entire body and for a moment he thought he'd start shaking uncontrollably. He took a deep breath and held it.

"Go ahead, Brad, eat it. Eat the cake." He then leaned over and in almost a whisper said, "Eat it all. The whole thing."

Brad turned toward his father. He could feel the tears stinging his eyelids.

"But I don't want the whole thing." He fought to hold back the tears from falling. "I just wanted another piece."

"Eat it all, Brad." His father's tone didn't change. "You wanted the cake, eat the cake. Start eating the cake, Brad."

With a trembling hand, Brad used the fork to slice a thin layer down the side of the cake. He let it fall onto the platter, cut off a small piece and placed it into his mouth. His stomach quivered with fear as he slowly chewed and then speared the remainder of the slice with his fork.

"You're never going to finish the cake eating so slowly, Brad. Take bigger pieces. Come on. This is what you wanted. Eat the cake."

Brad looked at the cake, his first tear dripping onto the quartz. "I didn't say I wanted the whole cake, Daddy. I just said I wanted..."

"I know what you said!" his father yelled. "I heard it over and over again. It's your birthday! You want more cake! Now eat the Goddamn cake!"

Brad turned toward Suelen who was quickly making her way into the living room as though the kitchen was on fire, his one hope for assistance vanishing as quickly as his craving for more cake. He looked around the kitchen, peering out each doorway, hoping his mother would appear to somehow save him from what was about to unfold. There wasn't a soul in sight. No one but he and the madman sitting beside him.

"But..."

His father leaned back and watched him. "No 'buts,' Brad. Eat the cake."

After forcing another ten bites down his throat, the buttercream was working its way up Brad's esophagus and resting at the back of his throat. With his eyes begging his father to allow him to stop eating, he finally gave up when the man's expression didn't change. He simply stared back with a smirk – a know-it-all look that, along with the previous swallow of cake, forced Brad to jump off the stool and run into the bathroom to barf every last bit of cake, and any birthday dinner he'd eaten, into the toilet.

After almost ten minutes of vomiting, he wrapped his arms around his stomach hoping that would help stop the spasms. He walked back into the kitchen where his father still sat on the stool now talking to his mother who stood on the other side of the counter. They both turned toward him when he reached the island.

His father rose from the stool and crossed his arms.

"Will you ever ask for more cake after I've said you'd had enough?"

Brad shook his head, noticing for the first time that there were tears streaming down his face. He wasn't sure whether they were from heaving so strongly, the sweeping sadness that had overtaken him while in the bathroom or the frustrating inability to fight back against a man who held his life, and apparently his every action, in the palms of his power-hungry hands.

And now, more than fourteen years later, he stood in the middle of his bedroom, hugging his stomach with the same frustration and inner turmoil he felt the day he was forced to make himself sick. Back then, there was no way to stop the inner turmoil. But today there was. He looked at the closet doors and nodded his head.

The heavy fog that had enveloped his soul, on many occasions and without warning, crept inside of him again. Like a Nimbus cloud filled with grief, heartache and inexplicable suffering, it drifted from somewhere inside his head and quickly spread throughout his entire body. It filled him with sorrow and hopelessness and no matter how hard he tried, nothing except for drugs could help him battle these feelings.

Just one more time to get me through this night.

He patted the vial so the white powder spread in a thin, straight line along the top of his hand. Looking out his window, he gazed at the midnight black creek and golden house lights dotting the landscape across the way. He held one nostril closed and sniffed the powder from the top of his hand, throwing his head back to ensure maximum effect. He pinched his nose and wiped the water from his eyes as he stepped back and sat down on the bed. As he tipped the vial again to spread more cocaine onto his hand, a strange feeling seized his body. He struggled to see through the window and into the darkness outside.

It wasn't the drugs or his anger making him feel this way. It was an odd sense that somewhere in the distance, there was someone watching his every move. He jumped up, shut off the light and squinted as once again he tried to see through the blackness of night.

Nothing.

It was too dark to distinguish any objects other than the lights on the other side of the creek. Still, the eerie sense that there were eyes glaring at him made his insides shiver. He grabbed the vial. With a trembling hand, he silently cursed the clouds covering the full moon, the only light that could've helped him see the line of powder he sprinkled along the length of the window pane.

CHAPTER 8

The cars were whizzing by, blurred objects soaring past his window like the rapids of the Colorado River he rafted with Mia on their trip to the Grand Canyon.

Tom drove the car over to the shoulder on I-95 between Greenwich and Stamford and put it in Park without shutting off the engine. In one hand he held a half emptied bottle of Cutty Sark, in the other hand, the gun he'd used to kill a man. He bounced the back of his head against the headrest, over and over, until the pounding made him nauseous and on the verge of puking. When he finally stopped, he glanced at the clock: 11:20 AM. Almost twenty-four hours since he shot a man in the chest. He moved his gaze to the rear view mirror and barely recognized the man he saw. His complexion was almost cadaverous, his eyes haunted.

What did you do? What the fuck *did you do?*

Tom pushed his head deeper into the leather headrest behind him. The brightness of the sun creeping around the windshield visor caused him to squint and made him feel more sick to his stomach. He swallowed hard to suppress the vomit. Not that anything would come up anyway. He hadn't eaten since yesterday morning. Not only had the discovery of Mia with another man, and his response, killed his appetite, but he was too scared to get out of the car and purchase food in a public place. His face was probably plastered all over the news. He figured no matter where he went, he'd be easily recognized and the cops would have him in handcuffs within minutes. *Never gonna happen. I'll kill myself before I go to jail.*

Jumbled images of Mia and the man he shot bounced around the inside of his skull. Her legs wrapped around his naked buttocks... his back muscles swelling with every thrust... her moaning for him to take her, take all of her... something she'd never done while having sex with *him*.

He closed his eyes and thought back to the first day they'd met. Friends of friends had set them up, and when she walked into the restaurant he felt an immediate attraction. He wasn't sure what turned him on the most. Was it the way her silky blonde hair fell over her sexy blue eyes? The subtle sway of her hips as she slowly made her way toward the bar? Or was it the vulnerability he sensed hiding beneath her expression of confidence? Whichever it was, he didn't care. From the moment he met her, he had an intense urge to have her in his bed and under his thumb.

"You're early," she'd said, placing her Michael Kors clutch on the bar.

He didn't know much about fashion, but he'd seen the MK initials all over those fancy designer television shows he'd flip through. This woman obviously had class, and it turned him on even more.

"I'm only early for people who matter." He smiled enough to show his perfectly straight, white teeth.

"Linda said you were smooth." Mia glanced over the bartender's shoulder at the selection of liquor. "I guess she was wrong."

Tom felt a twinge of anger deep in his gut. *Who the hell does she think she is?* He forced a smile. *She's playing with you. Let it go. Just play back.*

"Okay... guilty as charged."

Mia grinned and nodded to the bartender. "Can I get a Ketel One Cosmo, please?" She grabbed her clutch, popped it open and took out her wallet.

"No," Tom said, placing his hand on hers. Her skin was as soft as a rose petal. "It's on me. Your drinks... dinner... everything is on me tonight."

Mia gently shook her head and swept back the hair falling over her eyes. "Thank you, Tom. But I'd rather go Dutch tonight and split the bill. It'll make me feel more comfortable."

Holy crap. Who did Linda and Jamie set me up with? This woman's a bitch and a half. Maybe she has more confidence than I thought. I have my work cut out for me.

"Absolutely." Tom was getting excited just thinking about the ways he'd get her to break. "Whatever makes *you* comfortable makes *me* comfortable."

She raised her Cosmo and they clinked glasses. "To feeling comfortable," she said, her blue eyes staring directly into his.

"To feeling comfortable," he replied, forcing a smile.

This is gonna be tough.

It wasn't until their fourth date at the most posh restaurant in Scarsdale that he found a few cracks in her demeanor. The room was set for romantic dining: the soothing glow of Edison bulbs softly lit just a small bit of space on each table. White linen tablecloths held black silk napkins, upon which sat the finest of silver. A small crystal vase filled with fresh roses was placed in the center of the table, decorating the secluded space with stylish subtlety. The classical music was barely audible but loud enough to fill any awkward silences.

Tom had selected the restaurant with two goals in mind: to gently soften Mia's tough exterior while wooing her to the point of having sex with him. And as the night moved on, he felt more and more certain that both of this date's intentions were being met.

When he brought up family, Mia would glance away before responding. *Weak spot.* Anytime he'd asked about past relationships – same thing. She'd pause, smirk and glaze over the subject like a light breeze over a still creek. Nothing said, nothing left behind. Not even a ripple. *Scared of being hurt.*

Ha! He laughed to himself. This was probably the way his parents' relationship had started – a liaison of mutual respect until years of marriage brought his father to his knees, obeying every order his witch of a mother would discharge. Like a soldier to a general, his father lived under her rule, beneath a thumb that squished him like an overripe grape until he finally succumbed to a massive heart attack at the ripe old age of fifty-six.

At seventeen years old, Tom stood by his father's graveside, staring through his hate at the woman who had squeezed his father's heart until it stopped beating. He searched for evidence of a tear, some kind of indication that the General had the ability to let down her guard and feel something for the man she'd led around by a leash for the past twenty years. But all he saw was a stone-faced bully, the rotten bitch who would spend the rest of her days living off his father's money and cursing him for leaving her when she'd given all of her life to him.

Picking up the shovel of dirt and tossing it into the six-foot-deep hole, Tom swore to himself that he'd never end up like his parents. He'd always be the one in charge. He'd always be the General. No matter who he ended up with, he would be the owner of the leash.

"I like you, Mia," he said, surprising the both of them. Tom leaned forward and took her hand. He could feel her tense, but that only made him grip more tightly. It was as if the world around him had finally come into focus, everything so clear for the very first time, and he wasn't about to let it go.

She placed her fork down on the plate and gently placed her hand over his.

"I like you, too, Tom."

Tom's stomach was like a bouncy house – a giant blow-up castle with a bunch of screaming kids jumping around inside. *Play it cool, Tommy Boy, just play it cool.* He'd hooked the toughest, most beautiful fish in the sea and there was no way he was going to chance ever letting it get away.

And now here he was, ten years later, sitting in his car on the side of I-95 wishing he'd never thrown the bait into the water. Whenever he'd allow the reality of yesterday to strike him, he'd struggle with disbelief over what he'd done... and why.

The voice on the phone made it sound as though Mia was in trouble, like someone was preparing to harm her. So as he sped toward the house, he grabbed the gun from inside the glove compartment and placed it on the passenger seat.

"If anyone lays a finger on her, I'll blow their fuckn' head off," he'd yelled aloud to himself, his voice muffled by the air blowing in through the open windows.

But his mind was racing almost as much as the car itself, and though a flash of the thought "look before you leap" attempted to creep inside his head, he pushed away just as quickly. He pressed hard on the gas pedal until he screeched to a halt in front of the house.

His legs felt numb as he jumped out of the car, and he walked like a soldier across the street, over the lawn and up to the front door. To try not to alert anyone, he quietly unlocked the door, glanced around and then went in. Looking around, he tip-toed through the living room, dining room and attached office. Nothing. No one.

Was Mia even home? Did he fall victim to a prank call? Or did the caller lure Tom home to rob or even kill him? Tom held the gun by his chest with both hands. He was surprised by the absurd thought that if this weren't happening in real life, he'd probably make a great cop in a TV police drama series. He slid against the wall of the long corridor leading to the master bedroom, cautiously checking the kitchen, bathroom and guest bedroom along the way.

And then he heard it.

At first the sound was a whimper, a soft groan as if someone was in the midst of a nightmare, trying to break free from a faceless captor. But then it changed. It was a moan, a sound of rapture and delight, accompanied by rhythmic sighs of sexual pleasure. *What the fuck?* At that moment Tom fully realized what he was hearing. The horror of it froze him for a few seconds before he continued to glide against the wall until he reached the master bedroom. He silently pushed open the door and walked into the room, the sight before him inciting nothing but rage. His mind was in a frenzy and without thought, he lifted the gun, took off the safety and aimed the pistol directly at the man's back with both hands.

"Mia." Tom's voice was robotic, mechanical. "Mia!" His tone grew louder, the venom in his gut now burning his throat. "Mia!" He was yelling as his mind went numb, prohibiting any thought from entering or exiting. He felt a chill of adrenaline coarse through his veins.

"Who is he?" Tom shouted. "What's his name?" No answer. There was just screaming, crying and sobbing coming from Mia and the unknown man. He couldn't remember who the sounds came from or in what order he heard them.

"What's his name?" Tom shouted again, to no avail. His arms were like rods of steel. The pistol, still held in both hands, followed the motions of the nameless man currently trying to pull up his pants. It was when the man held up his hands and opened his mouth in an attempt to say something that Tom pulled the trigger. He wasn't exactly sure why that was the moment he decided to do it, but regret gushed over him like a waterfall the second he loosened his grip on the gun.

The man fell backward, knocking the lamp off the night table. Chaos inside Tom's head forced him to pull the trigger again, this time making the man stumble and bend forward until he toppled onto the bed beside Mia.

He heard her scream, "Dave!" before her hollow cries turned into bellows of anguish.

"Dave," Tom said, rushing toward the front door.

Whattya know, the asshole does *have a name.*

Tom took another quick glimpse in the rear-view mirror.

"*You're* the asshole," he murmured. "She didn't love you. You didn't love her. And now you screwed up your whole life for what?" He could barely understand his own drunken mumbling. "For *what*? A useless slut who never listened to you anyway? Why? Holy shit... why?"

He leaned his head back and let it fall to the side. He struggled to focus on his side view mirror and the action taking place behind him: three cop cars with flashing lights pulling up and braking so hard a wall of dust obscured his view. At first, panic shot through his entire body like someone was holding a taser gun against his gut. And then, as he glanced at the gun in his hand, the dread was brushed aside by a sense of calm. Within seconds it all became clear: he wouldn't allow anyone to win— not the cops, not Dave and especially not Mia.

Taking one last look out the windshield into the blue, cloudless sky, Tom saw a team of geese flying toward the Sound. *So lucky,* he thought, *to be able to fly. To be so free. To be able to escape. So lucky.*

He placed the barrel of the gun beneath his chin and closed his eyes, hoping he'd soon be as lucky, and as free, as the geese he so envied.

CHAPTER 9

There was one thing Scott Atwood knew for certain: after following Joel's spying tactics last night by using his own stargazing telescope to watch Brad snort more blow than a crack whore, it was obvious he *had* to include the All-American jock doc in his book. The best part was, the excitement of snooping on Brad and adding another character to his story made his writing juices start to flow.

After Brad had shut his light, Scott ran down to his laptop and found himself unable to type fast enough to keep up with his thoughts. Mia... Tom... Dave... Joel. They all came at him at once and he had to take deep breaths to keep calm enough to write the story properly and keep the details intact. The reader needed to know a little about each character and their flaws. Enough to get them hooked, but not give too much away. Of course he couldn't keep his readers hanging for too long, their reviews often made a point of that, so he decided Chapter 4 would be the perfect spot in the book for Dave to be murdered.

As far as the Sheehan kid, Scott wasn't yet sure how to handle that situation. He knew he'd have to find a way to get Brad's parents to discover the boy's addiction. But how? At what point in the story?

One step at a time. You wrote four chapters in one night. You'll figure it out.

Whatever he had to do to get his parents to find out, he'd do and leave the rest up to fate. His flurry of excitement grew as it became obvious that some stunning, edge-of-your-seat fiction would emerge from the situation, and he was prepared to spill every last drop of it onto the page. Of course, he didn't want another death or murder to occur.

Or did he?

It sure would make it more interesting. Death and murder always kept a reader reading. Always.

But no, he couldn't let that happen.

Or could he?

He knew his biggest feat would be changing up a shitload of facts within the novel before handing it off to Grace. After completing four chapters, it was more than evident there were plot pieces, conflicts and character qualities that hit too close to home. Sure, some stuff he'd made up, but large sections of the manuscript were based on reality. Anyone who knew him, hell, anyone who watched the news and then read his book would immediately realize that he was the cause of the chaos inside the once quiet and peaceful town of Scarsdale. He couldn't take that chance and was preparing himself to edit his work once it was done – significantly enough to ensure no one could link him and his actions to the book's plot.

Scott leaned back in his desk chair, clasped his hands and laid them on his chest.

The main character can't be an author unable to come up with an idea. It'll be a reporter. Yeah, some low-ranking journalist in need of a juicy story so he can finally get his byline in the spotlight. Maybe I'll change the Mia character to a man who's having an affair with his wife's best friend. And, Christ, there's no way I can have the jock doc be a drug addict. That would definitely raise suspicion. And now that I think about it, Joel was so attracted to this kid, I should probably make Brad a closeted gay guy whose father catches him in a compromising position with the quarterback of the local high school football team.

Yeah, I like that. I like that a lot.

For the moment, though, he'd have to keep writing things exactly as they happened. This would help him keep the facts straight and plotline on track from start to finish. He'd modify the telling components before sending out the manuscript, but for now he had to write the novel based on the facts – and, of course, some creative drama he'd invent along the way.

Holy shit! A work of fiction that's mostly non-fiction. Who would've thought...

Before he had a chance to finish that question, the pain in his right arm returned. He grabbed his bicep and squeezed, then rubbed it. *What the hell?* And there were the voices again, the yelling, the strange rustling. He knew there was something wrong. The problem was, he wasn't sure if it was physical, mental or both.

But what the hell was he supposed to do? Go to a doctor? If he did, what would he say?

"It hurts. Then it doesn't hurt. I'll be fine for a little while and then boom, out of nowhere, it feels like someone cut my arm off."

The doctor would probably scratch his chin, stick the stethoscope earpieces into his ears and hold the chestpiece to Scott's back. Then he'd ask: "Did anything happen that might've set it off?"

Yeah, I caused a murder and ruined the life of a lovely, beautiful woman.

"No. I can't think of anything in particular."

"Are there any other symptoms?" He'd move the stethoscope diaphragm to another sections of Scott's back.

I sometimes hear voices... and sirens... and screams. But when the pain subsides, so do the sounds.

"No, no other symptoms."

"Hmmm... well your heart and lungs sound good," the doctor would say, still unable to provide a clear diagnosis.

And then would come the MRIs and CAT scans, the prescriptions, the medical bills and the follow up appointments. No, he wasn't going to go through that. Unless the pain grew so intense that he couldn't strike the keys on his keyboard, he'd wait until the book was finished before even thinking about visiting any kind of a doctor.

With the pain slowly subsiding, he rubbed his arm some more and attempted to get his mind off his ailments by re-reading the last paragraph of Chapter 4. He smiled, completely satisfied with what he'd written and content with the fact that he'd soon have something to send Grace. However, his author's intuition told him it was now time to get the police more involved in the story. It was a distinctive mark of his novels, a characteristic that had always been praised by reviewers: including police procedural activity while giving the law enforcement characters full permission to express their emotions within the narrative. And this book would be no different. He just had to make certain that no matter the rank, color or gender of the primary law enforcement protagonist, the character had to be strong, smart, and above all else, sympathetic.

Ahhh... Detective Jordan.

Scott picked up his cellphone and speed-dialed Jordan.

Jordan answered on the first ring. "Mr. Atwood," he said with a smile in his voice. "Let me guess. You've just started a new book and need another ride-along or piece of juicy information to get you in the right frame of mind to write."

Scott laughed. "Ha! See, that's why *you're* the detective."

Silence.

"Let's try this again," Scott said, trying to keep the humor in his tone. "I said, 'see, that's why *you're* the detective.'"

"I'm sorry, Scott. Someone just handed me a message that I need to look into. We just have a lot going on down here."

Scott heard the gravity in Jordan's voice. "I'm sure you do, detective. If you remember, you and that blockhead, and I'm being kind by using that phrase, were questioning me on my front porch this morning."

"Yes, yes. Of course I remember. I'm surprised it took you this long to call." Scott smiled at the sharp sarcasm. "Don't tell me. You're looking for something story-worthy."

"Yes and no." Scott tried to figure out how to tiptoe around his words. "I was actually at Joel Peterson's this morning."

Silence. Then some rustling of paper.

"Peterson..." Jordan mumbled. "Peterson..."

"The gay agoraphobic who lives a few houses up from me."

"Oh, the guy –" Scott heard Jordan interrupt himself. "The agoraphobic. Yeah."

"Well, while I was there I found out Mia was staying with him. I wanted to offer her any help possible. She's going through a lot of shit."

Jordan didn't respond.

"I just thought," Scott continued, "we could get together like we usually do and talk a little bit. Maybe give me a thought or two on the case so I can play off some real-life events in my latest book."

Oh shit. Scott realized he might've just said too much. *Shut up before you give everything away.*

"Scott, listen," Jordan said. "I can't share the details until the lieutenant closes the case. I'm on my way to see Mrs. Blythe right now. I'll stop by before I leave the neighborhood."

Why is he going to see Mia? Did something happen?

"That would be great. We don't even have to talk about the case. Would love to just catch up." *Yeah, right.*

"Me too," Jordan responded, his keys jingling in the background.

"Before you go," Scott stammered, not wanting to spoil his chance of Jordan stopping by. "Is everything okay? Like I said, I'm working with Joel to try to help Mia get through this. If something happened, I'd like to be there for her to..."

"Since I'm on my way there now, I'll tell you the message I just got. But Scott, do *not* talk to anyone about this, including Joel and Mia, until after I've discussed this with them."

"Haven't I always kept your confidence?"

Scott closed his eyes tightly through three seconds of silence.

"Yes."

"That didn't sound very convincing, Darryl."

"It's just that this is such a high-profile case, I can't..."

Scott interrupted. "Remember three years ago at that Irish Pub downtown? You had one too many Dewars on the rocks and told me about the Freddie Jackson evidence? That he would most likely be arrested in three days but I couldn't tell a soul?"

"Yes, Scott. I remember."

"And I didn't tell a soul, did I?"

More silence. "Not that I know of," Jordan laughed.

"Darryl, I think I'm starting to get insulted." Scott crossed his fingers.

"Okay. I hear you," Jordan said. Scott heard voices in the background as though Jordan had a cavalry of cops behind him. "They found Tom Blythe on I-95 in his car with a self-inflicted gunshot to his head. He's dead."

Scott fell back into his chair and closed his eyes. Unable to speak, he waited for Jordan to continue.

"Gotta go. I'll see you in about an hour."

Scott shook himself from the impact of Jordan's words and opened his eyes. He clicked off his phone and threw it onto his desk.

Holy shit. I've now killed two *people. I'm a freakin' serial killer.*

That's when he heard Mia's voice again, sounding just like it did as he left Joel's house. Only this time he heard the muffled words a bit more clearly. He couldn't completely comprehend what she was saying, but he knew for certain that she spoke only three words. He spun his head toward the living room. No one. Then he stood up and walked toward the kitchen. Still no one.

"Hello?" he yelled. Nothing. "Mia?"

There was no reason she'd come here and there was no way she could get in the house. Was it possible she found out the role he'd played in the deaths of two men in her life and was somehow playing with his mind?

No.

Impossible.

But her voice had sounded so *real*, he was sure she was somewhere in his home, speaking to him.

"Mia?" he yelled again. "Mia, where are you?" This time he screamed the words.

Silence stared back at him.

"You're losing it, Scotty. You're absolutely fucking losing it." He walked back into his office and threw open the cover to his laptop. "But before you completely lose it, get this shit written."

He started typing with a fervor he hadn't experienced since writing his first bestseller, *In the Midst.* Tom's death was a tragedy, yeah, but that's what this book was about: tragedy, death and the effect one action can have on so many different lives.

Scott stopped typing and looked out the window and up toward the sky.

"Tom, millions of people are going to love this book. Isn't the pleasure of millions worth the lives of a few?" Scott started typing again. "I swear, I'll make Chapter 8 about you."

***

"Goddamn it, Sheila, you do shit like this all the time!" Scott held his cell phone in front of him, yelling at it as though it was his ex-wife. "Why can't you do it for me?"

"All the time?" Sheila asked. Scott almost felt her incredulity slap him across the face. "I help people move. I stage homes. I decorate mansions. I don't hire people to clean up murder scenes."

Scott sighed. Sheila was once again demonstrating just a few of the reasons they'd gotten divorced in the first place: Sarcasm. Privilege. Lack of imagination. He shook his head. *And she was the one who filed for divorce. What the...*

He smacked his head to stop his thoughts. He'd already wasted too many hours, usually while trying to fall back asleep at 3:00 or 4:00 AM, attempting to figure out why *she* would serve *him* with papers. Sure, they had their problems. He might have had a *dalliance* now and again, but he'd always given her everything she wanted. Coming up with a reason why she'd give that up was a futile task and now was not the time to pick a fight. He needed help. Scott took a deep breath and exhaled slowly, bringing the phone back to his ear and forcing a smile.

"Jesus, Sheila! I already told you that I'll take care of the cleanup part. But once it's done, I need a designer to go in there and rework the house. You might not be the easiest person to deal with, but you definitely know your shit when it comes to beautifying a house."

Silence. Then, "*I'm* not easy to deal with? *Me?*"

Figures, she didn't hear the compliment, just the jab.

"I take it back. You're easy to work with. Now can you help? I don't want to start interviewing decorators. You're the best and I'll pay you well, you know that."

Scott heard rustling on the other end of the phone and figured she was probably in the midst of getting her nails done or trying on a new pair of Prada pumps. She always loved spending his money and now she didn't even have to sleep with him to squander it.

"The whole thing gives me the creeps. I really don't want to redecorate a house where someone was murdered. Why don't you have Amanda do it? She's your faithful assistant, isn't she?"

"I let her go a few months ago. There wasn't much for her to do."

"Did you stop screwing her or did she stop screwing you?"

"Neither, Sheila." He pushed back his anger. "It was never like that with Amanda and you know it."

"Oh, then you're trying to get *Mia* into bed."

It's even worse than that, Scott thought. *I'm using her as the major protagonist in my book and need her to trust me and open up. Of course, if something were to happen between us...*

"Sheila, can you give me a little more credit than that? Mia is in pain. I have money. I'm trying to help –"

"Scott, please. We've been here before. Remember your first fling, Janet? Wait, was Janet the first or was it Melissa? No, Melissa was number three. I think Allison was the first. Yes, Allison. Doesn't matter. The thing is, you now expect me to believe you're doing this for Mia because you feel bad for her? Not because she's a beautiful woman whose lover is dead and won't have a husband once they catch him?"

Scott shook his head. With all the women he'd had, why was Sheila the only one who could squelch him into silence? She wasn't the most attractive of his conquests, that's for sure. Maybe it was her strength. Or maybe she reminded him of his mother, the only other woman against whom he could never win an argument.

Shit. Stop. Get back on track.

"Sheila, think about what you want. I know why I'm doing what I'm doing. This is the last time I'm going to ask. Will you help?"

"Really, Scott. It's creepy."

"Sheila, you liked Mia, didn't you?" He rolled his eyes as he heard her bark orders at the person manicuring her nails. Apparently there were unwanted streaks in the polish. "Sheila?"

"Yes, Scott. I did like Mia. Lovely girl. Just lovely. I feel terrible for her."

Yeah, I'm sure. "Well then, why can't you help? Just this once."

He waited and covered his eyes with his hand when the words he'd been waiting to hear finally came out of her mouth.

"What's in it for me?"

From the day they were married, this was the way most of their conversations had gone. To try and answer the question she just asked was fruitless, since anything he'd offer wasn't what she wanted to hear. It took him years to learn, but the only way to stop going around in circles was to answer that specific question with a question.

"What do you want?" He surrendered without a fight.

Scott listened to the nail spa's background chatter. It was jumbled noise, almost pandemonium-like and none of it made any sense to him. He wasn't even sure what he was hearing was English. He was about to ask her the question again when she spoke.

"The house in Key West," she blurted out.

"Sheila, you have *got* to be kidding me. There is no way –"

"Hold on, Scott. I don't *want* it, want it. I just want it for this winter. I've been too busy to make plans for my winter getaway and the house sits empty most of the time anyway."

Scott wanted to slam the phone down on his desk with such a loud crash that Sheila's eardrum would burst. She was asking for too much as she always did and he wasn't sure he could give in.

"Are you still there?" asked Sheila.

Scott heard an inkling of impatience in her voice. Her nails were probably dry and she wanted to leave the spa so she could get onto her next spending spree. He knew she didn't give a shit if someone had been murdered in the house or the floors were made from dog shit, if she got what she wanted from him, she'd do just about anything – as long as it wouldn't chip her nails.

"Yes, Sheila, I'm still here." It was time to surrender. Again. "If you get it done in the next five days, you get the house for the winter."

"Consider it done." He heard her car keys jingle. "I'll email you updates as things progress, along with the invoices, of course."

Of course.

Scott hung up the phone without even saying goodbye. Just like the old days, Sheila had taken advantage of his shortcomings for her own benefit. This time it was his need to spend his time writing and not wasting precious hours searching for an interior designer. Grace or Amanda would always handle those kinds of things for him. But now Amanda was gone because he'd made one too many passes at her. And there was no way he could call Grace. She'd just torture him about the manuscript, timing, printing and the rest of the bullshit her agent brain was addicted to.

But he realized he was going to need more help if he was ever to get this novel done.

Scrolling through the contacts on his phone, he searched for someone who might be able to help him find a new assistant. When the doorbell rang, his mind was jolted from thought so forcefully, he almost fell out of his chair. He'd completely forgotten that Jordan was stopping by. He let his pulse settle a bit before walking out of his office and making his way to the front door.

"Detective," Scott said, opening the door. He smiled and extended his hand.

"Author," Jordan countered, shaking Scott's hand. "Although you're looking a little pale and gaunt, it's nice to see you."

Scott led Jordan down the hallway and into the living room. "Geez. Nice to see you, too." He glanced into the bamboo-framed wall mirror before sitting down on the sofa across from Jordan. "Do I really look that bad?"

"Depends on what you mean by 'that bad.'"

"Not funny, Darryl. I've been under a lot of stress lately. I knew it was affecting me internally, but I didn't think *others* could see it."

Jordan unbuttoned the cuffs of his denim shirt and rolled up the sleeves. As he loosened the tie around his neck, he laughed. "Calm down, Scott. You just look a little tired, is all. No need to get all hot and bothered."

Scott pointed to Jordan's rolled-up sleeves. "Talk about hot and bothered."

"It's a thousand degrees out there."

"And you're wearing a denim shirt. Where's your coat? Did you leave it in the squad car?"

The detective let out a heavy sigh and shook his head. "You know I don't drive a squad car. I've been promoted to a Cherokee."

"Movin' up in the world."

"Not fast enough."

Mia, Tom and the murder case were hanging off the edge of Scott's tongue, but he held himself back. If he appeared overly eager to discuss it, Jordan would get turned off, maybe even suspect him of something. He took a breath.

"Want something to drink, detective? Water? Iced tea? Whiskey?"

Jordan gave a slight wave of his hand and let it fall on his knee. "No thanks. I'm good. The whiskey sure does sound tempting, but it's way too early." He glanced at his watch. "Way too early," he repeated, obviously trying to convince himself of his own words.

This was Scott's opening. He could see the fatigue on Jordan's face and hear it in the tone of his voice. It was now or never.

"Talk about looking tired, my friend. You look like you've been through a war."

"Just came from Joel Peterson's and spoke with Mia." Jordan turned toward the giant windows and gazed out at the creek. "Poor woman's been through hell."

Not wanting to interrupt Jordan's stream of consciousness, Scott kept quiet. He twirled a loose strand of thread hanging off the fringe of one of the sofa pillows to help keep him busy while trying to maintain his silence.

"I told her about Tom." Jordan continued looking outside. "Didn't say a word. Just stared right through me. No emotion. No tears. Nothin' in her eyes. She's hard to read, that one."

Scott nodded. He liked Darryl Jordan. He liked the man's dedication toward his work and envied his compassion. He never used words to show his empathy. No, that wasn't allowed – probably something they taught him in cop school. But he could see it in Jordan's expressions, the manner in which he spoke and the shape of his eyes that would often change right in the middle of a conversation. Maybe, Scott thought, the rumors about Jordan's drinking were true and he drank so much because his heart was too big for the pain he saw day in and day out.

Should I make him more of a main character in the book?

Slow down, Scott. One thing at a time. One thing at a time.

"So." Jordan turned back toward Scott. "You're writing a new book?"

"Yes."

"Have a title yet?"

"No."

"Can you give me the storyline?"

"No."

"For a writer, you sure don't use a lot of words."

Scott smiled. "Sorry, Darryl. My mind is all over the place."

"I can see that. So tell me why I'm here. You're not going to use this case in your book, are you?"

"Of course not," Scott answered without delay. "I would never. You know that. There are just a few things I wanted to ask you about that might be able to help me with the storyline."

"The one with no name?"

"Yes, Darryl. The one with no name." Scott took a deep breath. This guy's too smart for his own good. I can't get *anything* past him.

"Okay, but remember, even though I already spoke with Mia, I can't get into the specifics of the case until everything becomes public. It can't come out of my mouth. Got it?"

Scott was getting antsy. He needed more. Details he could use for his book and facts that would ease his worry. Hopefully he'd hear proof that they'd never be able to discover who made the call to Tom.

"I understand, totally. I just have a few questions that really shouldn't intrude on the confidentiality of the case." Scott scooped his notebook up from the side table and opened it to the first blank page. He decided to start off with a question to which he already knew the answer.

"How long was Mia seeing this guy who was killed?"

Jordan looked around the room as though he was looking for an answer he didn't want to find.

"One year."

"And Tom never knew until yesterday?"

Is he buying this? Does he know I know the truth and is just playing along?

"I can't answer that." Jordan leaned forward, elbows on knees and looked directly into Scott's eyes. "Now I have a question for you, Scott. You pretty much work from home every day, right?"

Scott nodded, his insides tightening like a fisherman's knot.

"You're looking out your windows, I presume. Taking breaks. Walking outside. Can you honestly say you never saw anyone go into Mrs. Blythe's home on a regular basis?"

Scott felt a wave of panic envelop his entire body. If Jordan taught him one thing while discussing his other books, it was that looking away from an interrogator was pretty much an admission, a confession of fear and lies. He returned Jordan's stare without blinking.

"Well, first of all, I'm not always home. I *do* have a life outside this house. Secondly, when I write, the AirPods go in the ears, the music starts playing and I'm lost for hours at a time. There could be a circus going on in my dining room and I wouldn't know it."

Jordan fell back into the sofa and let out a huge sigh. His crow's feet became less intense and the corners of his mouth moved up. It was easy to see he was loosening up and the decreased tension put Scott a bit more at ease. He forced himself to continue, afraid that stopping the questions might suggest guilt.

"Well, I'm surmising that if it was going on for a year, Tom would've done something way before yesterday if he knew about it." Scott held his breath. He had to find out if the police knew his anonymous call was the reason for Tom's actions. He exhaled and let the words flow like a river: "Why do you think it happened yesterday?"

Jordan shrugged his shoulders. "No idea. Really can't say. But based on what we've learned from neighbors, Tom's car was racing up the road and screeched to a stop in front of the house. I may be wrong, but that leads me to believe someone told him about what was happening and he rushed home to catch her in the act."

Scott's mouth was so dry his tongue almost stuck to the roof of his mouth. He attempted to hide his gulp. *Another sign he might look guilty.*

"Any idea who might've told him?"

He held his breath.

"No idea. Since we now have his phone, we'll check to see if a call came in around the time of the event. If one did and we can easily identify the contact, we'll have some sort of lead. If it was an unknown caller, it gets more difficult. We'll have to work with the cell phone company and go through the typical process of tracing a call. Depending on the type of phone used, serial number tracking, SIM card and a whole bunch of crap you don't want to hear about, there's a twenty-eighty chance we'll find the caller."

Twenty-eighty? Good odds, but I still don't like them.

"How long does that take?" Scott asked. "I mean, to track down an anonymous caller?"

Jordan shrugged again. "Could be days. Could be weeks. Could be never."

"Never, huh," Scott repeated, uncertain whether he was talking to himself or to Jordan.

"What does this have to do with your book? Not that I can give you any classified information, but I'd have thought you'd be prying for more info about the Blythes or other involved parties."

Scott forced a smile. "I don't know. This stuff intrigues me, I guess. It's a mystery, I write mysteries, I like to solve mysteries." He hesitated. *Watch what you say.* "Intrigue helps my creative mind create."

The detective slowly stood and walked to the French doors overlooking the creek. Scott stayed seated and kept his eyes on Jordan, watching him from behind, wondering what he was thinking.

"Right now I'm not concerned if someone did or didn't call Tom Blythe. It's pretty obvious why Tom Blythe did what he did and if the information that prompted his actions was delivered by a phone call, friend or foe, it doesn't really matter. He shot and killed an unarmed man." Jordan shook his head and turned around. "And then he shot himself."

Scott felt his entire body loosen. The call he'd made to Tom meant nothing to anyone but himself. This was good news. Very good news. Letting go of his tension allowed him to notice the look in Jordan's eyes and how they'd changed from those of a steady, clear-headed detective to a mournful, hopeless man.

There's that compassion again. I wonder if he still thinks it's too early for whiskey.

"So does that mean the case is closed?" Scott asked, silently praying for an affirmative response.

"Well, I'm ready to close it, but the Lieutenant is stuck on the phone call to Blythe. He wants that put to bed before we close the case for good."

Scott's panic returned. He had to change Jordan's focus from the caller to someone else. Anyone else. From out of nowhere, a thought crashed down on him, and before he had a chance to think it through, he blurted it out.

"Have you questioned Brad Sheehan yet?"

Jordan turned to Scott and blinked his eyes a few times before responding. "Who's Brad Sheehan and why are you asking?"

Scott took a deep breath. Knowing he couldn't hide his distress much longer, he used his anxiety to feign concern.

"Well, you know the way people gossip." He waited for some kind of response from Jordan. He got nothing. "So, Brad lives around the block. 4987 Merrill Street, I think. Anyway, he's a med student at Harvard and... well... I've heard he's... well, a user."

Jordan cocked his head. "What do you mean, a 'user?'"

"A drug user. Like cocaine, pills, stuff like that." Jordan stared at him, expressionless. "Which is kind of strange because he jogs the neighborhood every day like he's a star athlete or something. I don't know how you can be a drug addict and stay in shape like that."

Jordan slipped his pen and notepad from his shirt pocket as he took a few steps closer toward Scott. "So what does this have to do with the Blythes?"

Scott took a deep breath. "Well, first of all, I'm thinking if he jogs this neighborhood every day, he probably saw *something*."

"And second?"

"I'm not sure there's a 'second.' But drug addicts shouldn't be trusted." Jordan subtly nodded his head but Scott could tell he was losing the detective's interest. "I'm just saying, from a police procedural perspective, shouldn't everyone who might know something be questioned?"

Jordon rolled his eyes. "Oh, now you're a police procedural expert?"

"Thanks to you!" Scott quipped. He needed Jordan back on his side.

Jordan laughed. "You got that right." He opened his pad and clicked his pen. "And who did you hear this 'drug addict' story from?"

"You hear things at parties, neighborhood get-togethers, fundraisers. People talk. I'm sure they say things about me too." He looked down at Jordan's shoes. They were scuffed and the left one had a stain on it that Scott would swear in court was blood. "It's part of human nature. People are gossipmongers. They just can't help it."

Jordan slowly shook his head. "And with your AirPods in and hours lost in thought, you still see him jogging the neighborhood?"

Shit.

"Like I said, Darryl, I'm not *always* at my desk with my eyes glued to the computer. I see the kid running. I see birds in trees. I see cars pass by. I take walks up the block. I go to stores to buy food. Give me a break."

"Sorry, Scott. I'm just curious as to why you'd bring his name up now. I mean, if you suspect him of something, why wouldn't..."

"Whoa. I didn't say I suspect him of something. I'm just saying that I heard he takes drugs, I've seen him jog the neighborhood, up my street and past Mia's house." Scott felt his legs go numb. Did he just screw himself? He had to find a way to turn his accusation into an act of assistance. "I just thought maybe he saw or heard something on one of his runs. Maybe he knew Tom and called him while in a drug-induced state. It could be my creative imagination going off the rails like it usually does. I don't know. I'm just trying to help."

At that moment, Jordan's phone started to buzz. He grabbed it from his shirt pocket, tapped the display and held it to his ear.

"Jordan," he answered. A few seconds of silence and then, "I'll be right there."

He hung up the phone and slid it back into the front pocket of his pants. He then tucked his pen and notepad back into his shirt pocket and rolled down his sleeves. Buttoning his cuffs, he looked at Scott and blinked.

"I gotta go," he said. "I'll check on this Sheehan kid on my way out of the neighborhood. Thanks for telling me about it. I just wish you'd said something before now."

"I'm sorry, Darryl. Really. I didn't even think about it until we started talking."

Walking to the front door, Jordan tightened the knot of his tie. "No worries, Scott. The evidence we have pretty much makes this an open and shut case. I just have to follow up on every lead. But you know that... you write the books." He smiled, though it couldn't hide the deep red veins in the whites of his eyes.

Scott cleared his throat and put his hand on Jordan's shoulder. "How 'bout next time you come over for dinner, drinks and a conversation about anything but work?"

Jordan stepped onto the front deck. "You got yourself a date. Give me a call."

"Will do," Scott yelled as he watched the detective slowly get into his Cherokee, carrying himself like an injured man. *He's getting old,* Scott thought as he closed the front door. He then caught his own reflection in the window of the door and shook his head. *Holy shit, he's not the only one.*

He walked into his office and plopped into his chair. If Jordan kept pursuing the phone call to Tom, there could be a problem. Although he'd made sure to check for cameras at the dump of the store where he bought the burner, paid in cash and also provided the clerk false personal information, there was no way he could be a hundred percent confident that he wouldn't get caught. He tightened his lips and felt secure in his decision to push Jordan's focus onto Brad.

With what he saw Brad do last night, Scott knew that getting him and Jordan to cross paths could lead to something. Hopefully it would get Jordan to suspect Brad of making the call. *But how can I help move that suspicion along?* He'd have to wait until after Jordan met with the Sheehans before making another move. In the meantime, he first needed to let Mia know he was having her home redone so that she'd soon be able to move back in.

Maybe, he thought, *she'll thank me with more than a handshake.*

"Jesus Christ," Scott said aloud to himself. "You're in enough trouble. Keep it in your pants for a change, will you?"

He picked up his phone and called Joel.

"Hey," Joel answered, sounding half asleep.

"Hey, is this a bad time?"

"No, it's fine. What's up?"

"I have some news for Mia. I'm getting her house taken care of and I wanted to fill her in on the details. I'll need her keys and other stuff to make sure this goes smoothly. Think she feels like getting out of the house and coming over here for a few minutes?"

"Hold on a sec."

Scott heard Joel call Mia's name before some rustling began, Joel obviously holding the phone against his chest or another body part in order to muffle their conversation. After a few more seconds of holding, Scott was ready to take the initiative and just walk down the block without being asked.

"She'll be there in about ten," Joel said. The pitch of his voice had changed. He sounded a little lighter, as though being by himself was something he'd fantasized about for days. "Thanks, Scott."

"You're welcome," he replied and hung up.

Scott wasn't sure whether Joel was thanking him for helping Mia or for helping him get some alone time. Whichever it was, Scott knew there was only one person he was truly helping, and that person was himself.

CHAPTER 10

Holding the bottle of Chivas Regal in one hand and a shot glass in the other, Darryl Jordan tried to decide if throwing back a fourth one would be overdoing it. He thought through the day he'd just had, shook his head in an attempt to get rid of all the self-deprecating hollering inside his head, and quickly poured the whiskey into the glass.

Gruesome homicide scenes always put him on the verge of puking and the inside of Tom Blythe's Lexus was no different. The mix of blood and brain matter dripping off the off-white ceiling and upholstery forced him to turn away so he could keep his lunch down. That was probably the reason his partner had him meet him at the scene – Halleran loved to watch Darryl suffer and never stopped trying to prove he wasn't fit for the job. And as the whiskey flowed through his veins and calmed his nerves, *maybe,* Darryl thought, *that asshole is right.*

With his fingers still grasping the neck of the open whiskey bottle, he plopped down into his cushy armchair and looked around the one bedroom apartment. He'd lived there almost three years and the walls were as bare as the day he moved in. The empty pizza boxes were piled four high on the kitchen counter and his mail was scattered on the glass coffee table in front of the dusty flat screen television.

For a summa cum laude, you're pretty fucking stupid.

The vibration from his phone made him jump. *Who the fu...*

The caller ID read "Santana." He straightened his posture, took a slug of Chivas directly from the bottle and cleared his throat.

"Hey baby," he said. "How ya doin'?"

"Hey Daddy. I'm good. How are you?"

"Better now. Your voice always turns a bad day into a good one."

"Oh Dad. You're so sweet."

Darryl smiled. If there was one thing in this world that could make him smile, and most days there was only one, it was making his daughter happy – even if it was only with words.

"Talking 'bout sweet, you gettin' ready for your sweet sixteen party?"

"Yeah. I'm in my room right now. Becky, Sam and Brit are coming over to help me pick out the dress I'm going to wear. I can't wait." Darryl heard a doorbell ring in the background. "I think that's them now. I just wanted to make sure you're coming to the house on Friday before we go to the club."

Darryl took another swig of whiskey and closed his eyes.

"Depends on if your mom and her boyfriend let me in."

Before he finished the sentence, he knew he shouldn't have said it. He'd put Santana in the middle of his marital disputes too many times and every time it made her pull further away from him. *Another screw up.*

Before she had the chance to respond, he said, "I'm sorry, baby. Ignore that. I'm being stupid. Of course I'll be at the house. I wouldn't miss your pre-party for anything in the world."

"Are you okay, Daddy?"

He heard girl chatter somewhere in the distance.

"Yeah, baby. Just a hard day. I'm fine. Have fun and say hi to your friends for me. And tell Brit to make sure her skirt isn't too short, cause that girl don't have the sense God gave a lemon."

"Daddy! Stop! I'll tell them you send your love and can't wait to see them."

With those words, the background chatter increased in volume and the giggling he used to hear in the flesh had taken center stage.

"Okay, that's my cue. I love you, baby. See you in a few days."

"Love you, too, Dad. Gotta go." He was about to click off the call when he heard her say, "Don't forget to smile. Bye!"

"Bye, baby," he said to dead air.

He tossed the phone onto the sofa and took another swig.

"Smile? Again?" he asked himself out loud. "I think once is enough."

His mind was racing, thoughts scurrying around like bees in a hive. Sneaking Mia through her neighbors' yards to hide from the press; dropping her off with a friend who never leaves his house; Tom Blythe, and the expression on his face, or whatever was left of it, pushed up against the driver's side window; his conversation with Scott, words he could barely remember after he'd been offered a drink – the image of slugging down a pint of whiskey was the only thing he could think about from that moment on.

Then there was his meeting with Doug Sheehan. There was something so off with that guy, he felt it in his bones from the moment the man opened the door. With every word Sheehan uttered, Darryl saw shadows of the grim reaper – a dark, almost robotic alien lacking any sense of humor or emotion. And when he spoke of his son, it was as though he was referencing a new car or Rolex.

"Brad's behavior is exemplary," he'd said. "He does his schoolwork, he interns at Yale, and yes, he jogs around the neighborhood. Is jogging no longer allowed?"

Darryl was taken aback by Sheehan's tone. *This guy is one angry shit.*

"Mr. Sheehan, I apologize for any misunderstanding. I am not here to blame or implicate your son in any wrongdoing. My job is to follow up on any leads I have regarding what took place this past Wednesday. I was told your son jogs in that area so I thought maybe he saw something. That's it. No accusations here whatsoever."

Doug Sheehan stared directly into Darryl's eyes.

"Who told you he jogs in that area?"

Jesus Mother of Christ.

"I'm not at liberty to discuss this investigation with you, Mr. Sheehan. If your son is not home, then he's not home." Darryl pulled a business card out of his wallet knowing it was a waste of time. But that really didn't matter, it was creased and ripped anyway and slimmed down his wallet a bit. "If your son *does* have any information or would like to speak with me for any reason, here's my card. I'm available twenty-four seven."

Like an automaton, Sheehan continued to stare into Darryl's eyes while grabbing the card from his outstretched fingers.

"Thank you for your time, Mr. Sheehan."

As he walked away he considered going back to the station to finish some paperwork. And then the urge hit hard like it always did around this time of day, the cool burn of whiskey sliding down his throat, the smell of it as he lifted the glass, its flavor grabbing his tongue and not letting go. It was then he decided to skip the station and head home. The day had been long enough and he surrendered to the fantasy of making time for himself.

He took another shot of whiskey and stared at the phone lying on the sofa. He could still hear Santana telling him to smile, and so he did, again, even if it was half forced. She had it pretty good, his little girl, especially compared to Brad Sheehan. Sure, her parents were divorced and there was some friction between him and his ex-wife, Debra, but he knew she realized how much he loved her– especially since he always managed to sneak an "I love you" into every one of their conversations. From the day she was born, he and Debra decided that no matter what profession she desired, whether it be a ballerina, a physicist or even a cop, they'd back her every step of the way.

"I just want our little girl happy," Debra would say.

And Darryl's response was always the same. "That's all I want, too."

And they continued to repeat those words, even after their final fight that ended with a drunken Darryl stumbling onto the front lawn and Debra throwing three dresser drawers worth of clothes onto the grass beside him. It was the evening after spending the day at the murder scene of Melissa Jenkins, a well-known Scarsdale socialite who'd been bludgeoned to death by the boss of her landscaping crew. Streaks of blood swept across the walls and ceiling, a splattering of the red fluid creating a morbidly elegant design on the beige, lace curtains. The sight of the slaughter had made him run into the bathroom and puke, the horrific images tipping his mind and soul toward the edge of reality and imagination.

When he'd finally finished his investigation at the house, completed the paperwork and arrived home, he knew there was nowhere left to turn but the bottle. That was the first time he recognized he had an honest-to-God drinking problem. But that wasn't his only realization. He also started to fear he'd chosen the wrong career.

His extraordinary success in academia was a sign to just about everyone but himself that he should go to grad school, get a doctorate in a discipline he enjoyed, and bask in a fruitful and distinguished career. But his attraction toward becoming a detective and helping the community overpowered the pleading of others, especially his mother who'd complain that if he became a cop she'd be forced to spend her nights praying her only son would make it home alive and well each day.

He fought them all, the naysayers and realists, got his degree in criminology and then entered the police academy to continue his learning and gain investigative experience. Every now and then, usually while investigating murder scenes or dealing with suspects or victims on the brink of sanity, a drop of regret entered his bloodstream. Did he make the wrong decision? Should he have listened to those who told him to stay away from policework? Life, he continually thought, would probably be a lot easier filling test tubes with cancer-fighting serum or figuring out a code for the next technological breakthrough.

But those weren't the things that made his gut tingle with excitement or his mind race through the night with exhilaration as he tried piecing together obscure clues to his newest case. It was being a detective that made him want to get up in the morning... every morning... until recently.

As the Chivas fog started to meld within his thoughts, he let his head fall back on the chair and stared at the ceiling. He knew what the problem was: he cared too much. A job like his required the construction of a wall around his emotions; a sponge-like structure that could absorb his feelings and hold onto them until he could squeeze them out like filthy water into the grates of a street sewer or down a dirty drain. But that wall didn't exist and the increased sadness and excessive drinking quickly taking over his life was solid evidence of that fact.

He laughed at himself. Within two days he'd witnessed a man lying dead on a bedroom floor, another man with half his face blown off by a self-inflicted gunshot, a woman who could barely speak through her shock and here he was feeling bad for Brad Sheehan.

"Why?" he asked the empty room. "Why you feelin' bad for some smart, coked-up, rich kid?"

Even though he recognized his own sarcasm, the answer was clear as day – Doug Sheehan was the white version of his own father. He now understood why the man made the hairs on the back of his neck stand up. The mechanical way he spoke, the lack of emotion in his tone, the hollowness in his expression. It was his father, Jackson, a man who spoke only of the sanctity of work, the Lord and the expectations he had of his son.

"The Lord made you smart for a reason," Daddy would always say. "He don't want you breaking yo' back like me, lifting cement blocks and such. He wants you using your brain. And I'm gonna be makin' sure you use that brain. Every day and every night."

And that wasn't the worst part of Jackson's preaching. It was when he'd stand so close to Darryl that the boy would almost get drunk off the whiskey fumes oozing from the old man's breath. "And you ain't got no choice. As long as I'm here, I'm gonna be on you to make sure you make the most of what me, your mama and the Lord gave you. As long as I'm here, boy. As long as I'm here."

But he wasn't here for very long, dead at the age of 42 while driving drunk over the Hamilton Fish Bridge on his way home from a construction job. Although the car was found crushed against the steel girders with the driver's door open and a half bottle of whiskey in the passenger seat, Jackson's body was never found. The police concluded the door flew open upon impact and threw Jackson from the car and into the freezing cold waters of the Hudson River below. Darryl never bought that story, convinced his father crashed the car while intoxicated but staggered to the opening at the side of the bridge and jumped. He knew his father could never face his family and friends if charged with a DUI and the congregation would never let him live down going to prison. Darryl had calculated that it was either his father took his life of his own free will or the Lord finally told Daddy he was a rotten son of a bitch and it was time to free his family from his overbearing control.

Whatever the reason, when Darryl found out his father was dead, he felt more relief than sadness. Although he was only seventeen at the time and was elated that his father's daily sermons would finally cease, the fear, anger and resentment that went with years of incessant moralizing and preaching lingered inside of him to this very day.

Darryl closed his eyes and gave in to the booze. Tomorrow he'd deal with Brad Sheehan. Maybe even try to find him at his job. He'd also have to have a talk with Scott. Why *was* he asking so many questions about this case? Usually he'd inquire about the process or just tag along on calls to see how the investigative process worked while quizzing Darryl on how he'd find evidence and piece clues together. But he got a different feeling from Scott about the Blythe case. He was asking different kinds of questions, more personal and specific. Something wasn't right. Was it because the murder happened so close to his home or was it something else? Could he somehow be involved in this?

"Stop, Darryl. You're reachin' now."

He let his eyes close and promised himself that for today, he was done – done working and done thinking. His mind had had enough and it was time to pass out and sleep it off, hoping that when he awoke, the thrill of being a detective would somehow return.

CHAPTER 11

Mia walked around the perimeter of Scott's office, every so often running her index finger along the spine of one of the thousands of books filling the bookcases. Scott watched her every movement, mesmerized by her subtle beauty, which seemed to grow each time he caught her lost in thought. She seemed slightly dazed, but lucid enough to walk down the block to his house and inspect his bookcases.

Her hair was pulled back, exposing her high cheekbones and small yet perfectly proportioned nose. Without any makeup, her lips were plump and had a slight blush, like the petal of a fading rose. The blue tank top she wore hugged her slim torso and perfectly shaped breasts, making it difficult for Scott to stop staring. Her tight blue jeans created the same problem for him, and if the current situation wasn't as dire and morbid as it was, he'd be wooing her with bullshit lines and extravagant gifts until she finally gave in to his hidden charm. But things *were* dire and morbid and ironically, it was all his fault.

"Mia, would you like some water? Tea? Coffee? Anything?"

She shook her head.

"I'm surprised Joel let you come over. He seems very protective."

A faint smile crossed her lips. "I think we both needed a little break from one another." She brushed a few wisps of hair from in front of her eyes. "I have no words to describe how great he and Martin have been. But we all need some space. So thank you for inviting me over and giving us that space."

"Of course," Scott mumbled.

Mia continued to meander along the edge of the room, stopping when she reached the section of the bookcase that held copies of Scott's books.

"Do you read these?" she asked, pointing to his titles. Her voice was hushed, as though trying to keep a secret.

Scott was silent. He'd never been asked this question before and didn't have one of his pat answers at the ready. He cleared his throat to give himself more time.

"Well, I wrote them. Why would I read them?"

Shit. Was that rude?

"To see if you enjoy them."

I'm sure I'd enjoy them. I wrote them, for God's sake. They're perfect.

"Well, that's a very interesting question. Maybe I'll consider reading one of the earlier ones... just to see if it's as brilliant as I remember it."

He smiled. She didn't smile back.

"How do you come up with your ideas?"

Scott almost choked on his saliva. He swallowed hard. *Did she know?* He cleared his throat.

"That's a secret I'll never give away." He was embarrassed at the way his voice quivered as he waited for her to point and start screaming accusations at him.

"Which is your favorite?"

Scott gulped again. *"Dying to Tell."*

"Mine, too."

"You've read my books?"

The look of astonishment on his face caused one corner of her mouth to lift and almost smile.

Her voice was still subdued as she answered, "Of course. You're a great writer *and* you're my neighbor. *Dying to Tell* was a great book. Really, they're all great books."

"I feel honored, Mia. Truly honored."

Pangs of conscience and self-condemnation, something he hadn't felt since this whole thing started, crawled inside his gut. His imagination started to run wild. He pictured himself vomiting all over his desk and not having an explanation to offer – other than that he was the instigator behind her dead husband murdering the love of her life.

Stop!

He rose from his desk, walked to the loveseat by the window that overlooked the front yard and sat down. Hoping she'd follow his lead, he patted the seat cushion beside him. He couldn't take his gaze off her blue eyes as she strolled toward him, gently took a seat and slid her back up against the sidearm.

"No tea? Coffee? Iced..." He stopped asking when she shook her head. "Okay. Well, there are a few things I wanted to talk with you about. First, I'm taking care of getting your house cleaned for you."

Mia's expression went from inquisitive to vacant as though reminding her of the incident had pulled the essence of her soul out the corners of her tear-filled eyes. Her face was pallid and her lips trembled as she picked at the seam on the leg of her jeans. Scott placed his hand on hers. Her skin was softer than he'd imagined.

"I know this is difficult, Mia. I know. That's why I want to take care of it for you. There's a special type of cleaning crew that handles these kinds of things. When you go back, it'll be like new. I promise." Her lack of response made him worry she was about to break down and he'd have to walk her, if not carry her, back to Joel's. "I'm not sure if you know, but my ex-wife is a famous designer, and she'll be in charge of making sure that nothing looks... well, that everything appears... I should say, she'll make it like..."

For a writer, you're pretty pathetic at finding the right words.

"I understand what you're trying to say. And I can't thank you enough," Mia interrupted, lifting her gaze and looking Scott directly in his eyes. It was at that moment he understood the true meaning of one's "heart melting." "But I'm not sure I'll ever be able to step foot in that house again."

Scott lightly tightened his grip on her hand. "I get it, Mia. Though I could never understand what you're going through, I do understand your hesitance. I'm sure everything is just too raw right now and you don't want any reminders of the past few days. This is going to be a process. A very slow process. And I, like Joel and your other friends, are here for you."

Mia turned her gaze out the window toward the yard.

He continued. "I also want to take care of any expenses you might incur. Like if you'd rather stay at a hotel for a while rather than at Joel's, I'll pay the bill. Or if you have to get an attorney. I have one in particular at my beck and call. I can set you up with him and pay his fees. Whatever you need, I'm here for you."

Mia placed her other hand on top of his. The touch of her fingers moving on his hand sent a shiver up the back of his neck. He saw the pain in her eyes, in the delicate lines around her mouth. That recognition of conscience started to return and he pushed it down with the force of a jack hammer. There wasn't any time for that shit.

"I can't thank you enough, Scott. But I'm not sure why you're doing this. I mean, we've been neighbors for years and have only spoken to each other every now and then. I truly appreciate everything you want to do for me, I really do. But I just don't understand *why* you're doing them."

The word blasted into Scott's head as loud as a grenade blast: *Guilt!*

"Because I'm a nice guy?"

Mia kept her eyes on him without saying a word. She was waiting for an honest answer.

"Okay, maybe because I *want* to be a nice guy? Seeing what you're going through makes me realize that I have to start helping people and give a little more. I don't need to hoard my money for heirs that don't exist or charities I don't believe in. I want to use it to help real people... people like you who shouldn't have to worry about anything other than getting through a horrific time in their lives."

As she leaned over to kiss his cheek, Scott felt paralyzed. He didn't move when she wrapped her arms around him and laid her head on his shoulder. When he smelled the faint scent of his favorite fragrance, Chanel Coco on her neck, his sexual appetite rose along with the bulge in his pants. It brought him back to the *Dying to Tell* launch party at the Waldorf where after a few too many scotches he found himself having sex with one of Grace's junior editors against the woman's room wall. All he could remember from that brief encounter was the suppleness of the young woman's breasts, the odd fragrance of her sweat mingling with the Chanel Coco behind her ears and a peculiar desire for his wife to enter the bathroom so he could show her what real sex was like.

But Sheila never came in and Grace fired the junior editor that night as she exited the bathroom door. She'd apparently been waiting for them to finish.

"And if you weren't my number one cash machine," Grace yelled at him, "I'd fire your ass, too!' She wiped the lipstick off his mouth and pushed him down the hallway. "Now get back to your party and act like a decent, grown up human being."

He could hear her whisper *fuck!* to herself as she gazed into the lobby window, fixing her hair in its reflection and shaking her head.

And now, all he wanted to do was kiss the curve of Mia's neck and then slowly move his lips toward her mouth. Strands of her hair brushed along his face and he fought the urge to sweep them away, knowing it would only lead to him making a move he'd most certainly regret. With the sound of Grace's chilling words from the last encounter echoing in his head, he sat still, almost incapacitated, and waited for her to lean back against the sofa.

Does she want me to hug her back? Does she need physical contact to make her feel better? Would she want me to touch her hair?

Before he could find any answers, Mia slowly backed away and sat up straight. She wiped away the tears streaming down her face and grabbed a tissue from the side table to press against her runny nose. She grabbed another tissue and tried to gently clean the smudges of mascara she'd left on his left cheek. He didn't say a word, letting her make any move she wanted without egging her on.

"I'm sorry," she said, sniffing and attempting to hold back more tears. "It's just so nice of you. And I don't know what to say, other than 'thank you.'"

Scott shook himself loose from his paralysis and forced a smile. "No need to thank me. And I was thinking about something else."

Mia swiped the tissue across her nose and took another from the box. "What? What else were you thinking?"

"I'm sure there are a lot of legal things you need help with right now. Tom's will, inheritance, property ownership and a whole host of other things. The attorney I was talking about before, Larry Hindman, has a firm in Manhattan. He can handle all of that for you. My thought was that we go into the city so you can meet with him *and* to get you away from here for a little while. I think you need a break."

Scott could see the glaze reappearing over her eyes. He feared he was going too fast, pushing too hard. What was his problem? Why did he always do something to make women despise him?

"I'm not sure I'm ready yet," Mia said, now gazing out the window.

"I totally understand, Mia. I'm sorry. It was really just to get you away from here for a few hours. Change your surroundings and get your legal issues taken care of at the same time. Kind of killing two birds with one stone."

Oh shit. Did you actually just use the word "kill?"

"Let me think on it?" Her voice was almost a whisper.

"Of course," Scott said. Her response gave him some hope. "Take your time. You can let me know tomorrow. And if you'd rather go on Sunday, we can go on Sunday."

"Thank you again," she said. She stood up, took a key on a ring from her jeans pocket and handed it to him. "And here's the key to the house." She kissed his cheek again and started to walk toward the front door. Then she suddenly stopped, turned around and walked back to Scott. She gently touched his face with the back of her hand. "Thank you, Scott. Everything you're doing means a lot to me."

"It's my pleasure, Mia. Please know that."

After he closed the door behind her, he walked straight to the back deck and scanned the creek. It was eerily quiet. Not one raft. Not one swimmer. Not one duck or goose. Something wasn't right. This time of day, the creek would usually have at least a dozen people discarding their workday frustrations by trying to raft their way to happiness.

But today there was nothing, no one, not a sound. And although it was still almost eighty degrees outside, the sight made Scott unnerved, a feeling that intensified when he heard a woman's scream... and then another... and another. He leaned over the deck railing and darted his head in all directions. Nothing. He looked down into his own yard, silently praying he'd see someone, something, even a murder taking place that would help prove that these screams weren't coming from inside his head.

But there was no murder. There wasn't even a single human being. Just an empty yard, with emerald green grass and a baby squirrel running into the perfectly landscaped rhododendrons.

He held his head with both hands. "Holy shit! What the fuck is going on?"

The screams persisted, but lessened in intensity as he ran to the wet bar, almost tripping over the living room coffee table to get to the scotch. He barely finished dumping it into the glass before gulping it down at once. He grabbed the bottle of scotch and started to fill the glass again, his hand shaking so much he almost spilled the liquor all over the bar counter. When the glass was finally full, he finished its contents with two swigs. The screams faded a little more with each one.

"You need a shrink," he whispered to himself. He poured some more scotch and fell onto the living room sofa. Who the hell could he talk to about these things going on in his head? There was no one to confide in or confess to and he began to feel an overwhelming sense of self-pity at how alone he was in the world.

That's when it hit him: the screams were his punishment. Whether it was the God he never believed in or karma finally rearing its ugly head, he was certain that he was being condemned for his actions. He couldn't make any sense of it and suddenly lost the strength to try. The only thing he knew for sure was that he was on track to losing his mind and if he didn't get help soon, he'd be writing his novel in the loony bin.

He took another gulp of scotch and pushed himself further into the fluffy down pillows lining the sofa, waiting for the liquor to wash over his mind and dissolve his thoughts into an endless river of sleep.

CHAPTER 12

Other than almost getting hit by a bus while crossing York Street yesterday, Brad could barely remember the last day and a half. His mind was focused on one thing: Felicia.

Although it had only been three months since he'd last seen her, it felt more like three years. He ached to hold her again, smell her hair, rub the silky skin of her back as she lay her head on his chest.

He looked at his watch: 4:01. Where was she? Did she lose her nerve? Was she worried that seeing him would only bring back the memory of that horrible day at the clinic? Brad instinctively went to grab his phone from his back pocket when he remembered he'd left it at home.

Shit.

He was halfway to Yale that morning when he reached for his phone to call his Harvard housemate Jimmy. It was then he realized his phone wasn't in its holder and he started to freak out. *Where is it? Did I bring it? Did it fall on the floor?* And then the realization of where he'd left it hit him like a sledgehammer. He'd placed it on the counter next to the sink while shaving and never took it back with him into the bedroom. He was too far into the drive to turn around because if he did he'd be late, something he was sure his father would hear about. And that's when he remembered he hadn't reset the phone's privacy and security settings.

Holy mother of shit.

He'd never finished securing his lock screen with his fingerprint and now his new phone was unsecured, open for public view. The palpitations in his chest made him cough and the sweat pulsed out of every pore on his back. His shirt was wet and he thought he'd have to pull over onto the shoulder of the highway to quell his panic.

He took a deep breath. And then another one. At this point, all he could do was hope that luck was on his side and his parents and Suelen would keep far away from his section of the house. His odds were fifty-fifty, so he said a quick prayer to help his chances and turned up the radio to try and keep his mind occupied.

He checked his watch again: 4:03. It was close to rush hour and the traffic on York was getting busy. The people who worked in the buildings that made up the Yale Health complex were starting to leave for the day, finding their cars in the lots or getting onto the buses that would take them away from the sadness and suffering they'd dealt with their entire 12-hour shift.

For a few moments he pitied them until he thought about his current situation. He had his own shit to deal with, primarily the fact that Felicia was nowhere to be seen. He looked up and down the sidewalk, across the street. He even tried looking inside the windows of the passing cars.

No Felicia.

The excitement that had helped him get through the day was dissipating at a rapid rate. Cursing himself for leaving his phone at home, he ran his fingers through his hair and grabbed hold of the ends. The tug on his scalp felt like a fair punishment. *Of all the days to forget your freakin' phone, it had...*

"Hey."

The gentle voice came from a short distance behind him. His heart pounded as he spun around to see Felicia walking toward him. She slowly removed her sunglasses.

"Hey," he said back, trying to keep his exhilaration in check.

To his amazement, she appeared more beautiful than even the first time they'd met. He took her in with his gaze, looking her up and down like a blind man seeing for the first time. The black, high-waisted suspender skirt she wore highlighted her elegance and curves; the leopard-patterned ankle boots showed off her stunning legs and penchant for style. Her hair, strawberry blonde waves of silk, fell on his favorite shirt of hers, a Breton stripe, the one they bought together in Boston that hugged her in just the right way. She looked like a model ripped from the pages of Elle. He couldn't take his eyes off her, watching her every move, feeling as if it would take forever until she reached him. His heart beat as fast as a hummingbird's. He took a deep breath.

"Hey," she said again, her arms reaching out to hug him.

Brad gently put his arms around her, hugging her as though he were holding on for dear life. He kissed the crook of her neck and laid his head on her shoulder, smelling the scent of her skin that he'd only been able to fantasize about for the past three months.

"Hey," he whispered in her ear. "You look beautiful."

She hugged him tighter. "You *feel* beautiful."

After another minute, he loosened his grip and stepped back so he could stare at her again. "I thought you changed your mind," he said. "You're always early, so I figured when —"

"Didn't you get my text about the accident on 95? It took me *forever* to get here."

Brad looked to the ground. "I got a new phone and left it at home by mistake," he said, shaking his head. "Don't ask. My mind hasn't been working so well lately." He looked directly into her eyes. "It's been focused on seeing you."

She smiled with a tinge of embarrassment. "Same here."

The honking of the horns and parade of people walking up and down the street started to make Brad uneasy.

"Let's get out of here," he said, gently grabbing her hand. "How 'bout we go to O'Neill's and have an early dinner?"

Felicia squeezed his hand and put on her sunglasses. "I'm up for anything."

It was too hot to sit outside and since they wanted privacy anyway, they had the waiter sit them in a corner booth in the back of the restaurant. There were three patrons sitting at the bar and only four or five other tables where people were busy eating their meal. The only light in the restaurant was that coming through the slatted blinds of the floor-to-ceiling windows, far away at the front. Perfect, Brad thought, settling into the booth cushions, for a romantic encounter.

After they ordered their drinks, he placed his hand on top of Felicia's.

"I'm not going to ask how you've been doing," Brad said. "That would be a stupid question. I'll just guess from the fact that you wanted to meet that you're doing... well... at least a little better."

"I'm not going to lie," Felicia responded, looking at their clasped hands. "It was tougher than I thought it would be." She took a sip of chardonnay and attempted to hold back tears. "It's so hard to explain. Like I lost something I never had... a part of me that was taken away but of my own free will. I just... I couldn't..." Brad gently wiped the tear from her cheek with the back of his hand. "I'm sorry. I told you it was hard to explain. I can only say it was, and still is, a deep sense of loss and guilt."

Brad placed his other hand on top of hers. "I get it," he whispered. "I understand. Not from your perspective, but from my own. The baby was inside of you, not me. So I can't comprehend what you're going through. I can only say I feel a sense of loss and guilt also. And I pray every night that it will go away... or at least get easier."

Felicia traced her finger around the rim of her wine glass. "It hasn't gotten easier yet. But what I can be sure of is that I realized that not seeing you was only making things worse."

She looked up at him and didn't say a word, making him feel as though she was absorbing every inch of his face.

"A while? Almost three months, to be exact," Brad feigned a laugh. "That's a long time to figure out you missed me."

"I missed your from day one," she said. "It just took me this long to work some things out in my head."

Brad brought her hand to his lips and kissed it. "Like what things?"

"Can we not talk about that right now? Let's just say I'm trying to sort them out the best I can and, well, here we are. Let's talk about something else. Are things any better between you and your dad?"

He turned away as though a tray of dishes had crashed in the kitchen.

"I'm sorry," she promptly said. "I didn't mean to—"

"No ... no... it's okay." Brad took a gulp of his Corona Light. "He's still the man who only cares about two things, money and pushing me to my limits."

"I'm so sorry, babe."

"Don't be. Do you think he ever asked about how you were doing? Shit. He never asked *me* how *I* was doing. All he ever talks about is my future and how I can't let anything get in the way." He took another swig of beer. "And, of course, he reminds me just about every day that if it wasn't for his bank account, I'd be doomed to a life of poverty and failure."

"Wow. I was hoping he'd changed... especially after what we'd been through."

"He can't change. Doesn't know how," Brad said, stroking her hand. "So my plan is simple. I'll use him for his money. I'll do what I have to do to keep him happy. In the meantime, you and I will see each other as often as we can, and once I'm done with med school and start my internship, we can start our lives together. If I really bust my butt, it'll be only two more years instead of three. And while I'm doing that, you can get that art studio up and running. What do you think?"

Felicia took a sip of her wine and then another. Brad felt her hesitation. He rubbed her hand and intertwined his fingers with hers, hoping it would help her say the words he wanted to hear.

"What I think is that all I want to do is be with you. But I just... I'm not sure how that's supposed to happen while we're sneaking around and not being able to live our lives the way we want to. It's obvious your father doesn't want you to have a personal life, especially with me because of everything that's happened."

"Don't say that!" Brad protested. "It's not *you*, it's anyone."

"I know. I know. But knowing your father, I can guarantee he's convinced himself that I'll manipulate you through guilt and ruin your life." She glanced around the room. "It's sad that thought even has to cross my mind, but it's better we're prepared for his craziness so that we know how to manage it." She sighed and brushed away the strands hanging in front of his eyes. "I'm not even sure what I'm saying or what I'm supposed to say, other than I love you and I'll do whatever it takes to make this work. I just get so angry when I think about how he uses his money to control you."

"I'll take 'I love you' and leave it at that. One way or another, we'll make this work. I swear." Brad kissed her hand. "Now let's get off the subject of my father before I lose my appetite."

Felicia laughed. "Okay, I've seen you lose your patience, your marbles and even your phone. But I've never seen you angry enough to lose your appetite."

Brad leaned over and kissed her softly on the mouth. "And hopefully you never will."

***

By the time Brad pulled into the driveway, nighttime had descended, triggering the automatic spotlight above the garage to turn on and shine directly onto the hood of his car. His time with Felicia was so tranquil and enjoyable, he didn't want to spoil his mood by going inside where he knew his parents would be waiting to grill him about his day. So he waited for the spotlight to turn off and sat in his car listening to the CD Felicia had burned for him about a year ago. It contained all of his most treasured '80s tunes, and as he leaned back in his seat, his favorite Phil Collins song, "Take a Look at Me Now" began to play.

The lyrics brought tears to his eyes. The fact that he'd almost given up on the one person who knew him like no one else hit him hard. He made a vow that he'd never let that happen again. Felicia was the woman for him and no one would convince him otherwise. Screw his father. Screw his spineless mother. Screw everyone else. He'd become a doctor and whisk Felicia away to a place where they could live their lives exactly the way they'd planned.

"Just two years," he mumbled to himself. "Just two more years."

With the car windows open, he closed his eyes and tried to let the music fill him from the inside out. But there was an imperceptible nagging crawling through him. Something just wasn't right. The air felt *too* still, as though it was waiting for something to fill the negative space. He lowered the music and stretched his neck to listen. The front yard outside was dark and silent. No crickets. No cicadas. Nothing. The humidity hung so heavy it felt like a weight sitting on top of his head. He silently wished for a breeze, a sense of life to appear from somewhere, anywhere. And suddenly, as though the God of Bad Karma had heard his prayer, his father emerged from around the path of hydrangeas leading to the front door.

The man didn't say a word. He simply looked at Brad, lifted his left arm and motioned with his index finger to "come here."

Brad turned off the radio and got out of the car. The churning in his stomach worsened with each step he took closer to his father. He'd never seen the man wearing this expression before. It was somewhere between anger, hatred and shock. Before Brad reached him, his father did an about face and without a word walked toward the front door. Brad followed, using every ounce of energy he had to stop himself from turning around, jumping into his car and driving straight into the blackness of night.

The walk to the door was as long and arduous as a murderer's journey down the green mile. *The only problem is*, Brad thought, *I'll be alive when my walk is over.*

He trailed his father by only a few feet until they both entered the house. His first sight was that of his mother sitting in one of the two leather wingback chairs facing the sofa. Brad was about to say "hello" when his father slammed the door and pushed him toward the couch.

"Sit down," the man said. "On the sofa so we can both look at you."

Brad's heart leapt into his throat when he saw his cell phone on the pedestal table between the two chairs. Next to the phone, laid out neatly on a canvas placemat, were his Xanax, Oxy, Cocaine, vape inhaler and other pills – even the diazepam he'd forgotten he'd had. Although his legs were wobbly with fear, he used all his strength to make his way to the sofa and fall onto the perfectly positioned pillows.

Images of his bedroom flashed through his mind: clothes hanging out of dresser drawers, sneakers and cleats thrown about, papers from his desk scattered around the room. For his father to find all the items that now sat on the table, he must've ransacked the room like a burglar searching for a fortune. And apparently, he'd found one.

Brad looked up from his clenched fists and glanced at his mother. Her head hung down, her eyes staring at the tapestry covering the floor. Silent, as always. Once again he was on his own.

His father crossed his legs and broke the silence.

"We had an interesting visit today from a Detective Jordan," he said.

Brad's mind worked quickly, trying to recognize the name. Nothing. He shook his head.

"Never heard of him."

"He's the detective in charge of the Blythe fiasco on Anderson Court. The name doesn't ring a bell?"

Again, Brad shook his head. The trembling within his gut increased in intensity. The man in front of him was too controlled, too casual. It brought flashbacks of his high school football games as quarterback. Those few seconds prior to the center snapping the ball, when the defensive tackle would give him a smile before ramming through the offensive linemen and tackle him, practically burying him in the turf. Right now, his father's tone was the smile, but he knew the crushing tackle was not far behind.

"At first Detective Jordan wanted to learn if we knew anything about Mia and Tom Blythe. Anything that could help the investigation." He turned to his wife, who continued gazing at the floor. "Of course we didn't, since we rarely ever spoke to them. Honestly, I wasn't even sure of their names until I saw the story on the news." He feigned a laugh and glanced at the table covered with pills, drugs and a cell phone. "A whore and a lunatic living only a few blocks away. Did you ever speak with either of them?"

Brad shook his head, rubbing his fingers together, trying to breathe.

"The detective said he heard your jogs brought you down Anderson Court. Right past the Blythes' house to be exact. He thought you might've seen something the day of the incident. Did you see anything, Brad?"

"No," Brad mumbled. He cleared his throat. "No."

"Well, while he was here, we tried calling you." He pointed to Brad's cellphone on the table. "Suelen was upstairs and heard it vibrating in your bathroom, so she brought it down to us."

Brad looked at the phone and scanned the drugs. He closed his eyes and silently begged for the monster to stop torturing him. *Just get it out! Say it already!*

But his father sat calmly in his chair, expressionless, and kept talking.

"At that point, I told the detective you probably left your phone here in error and that if you knew anything, we'd have you get in touch with him." He uncrossed his legs and leaned forward, his elbows on his knees. "Is there any reason for you to get in touch with him?"

Brad felt his muscles tremble. He didn't know what the man wanted him to do. Admit something? Fight back? Say the drugs were someone else's? What the hell was he waiting for? He knew his father had already planned how this conversation would end, so he kept quiet and waited.

After about another minute of silence, without a sound or movement from his mother, his father swiped Brad's cell phone and held it between his palms.

"The first thing I did"—he turned toward his wife—"the first thing *we* did was look at your emails and texts."

Duh, Brad wanted to scream. *You're holding my phone. I'm not an idiot!*

"And we saw texts between you and Felicia, the girl we told you to stay away from." He pressed the button on the side of the phone so the display lit up. "I believe that's where you were tonight, with Felicia? Am I correct?"

Brad nodded. The burning in his gut heated up as his fear turned to anger. He knew he was being played, the man in front of him spilling hints of accusation without saying what he was really thinking. Brad's heart pounded, wanting to yell but not wanting to give in to the lunatic's game. The best he could, he hid a deep inhale and stared into the man's eyes.

"I see." His father pointed to the drugs, moving his index finger in a circular motion as though Brad wouldn't know what he was about to bring up. "Well, after we discovered you disregarded our arrangement regarding Felicia, we thought it necessary to go into your room and see what else you might be keeping from us." He continued pointing toward the table. "As you can see, we've discovered a few more of your disgraceful secrets."

His voice was getting grittier by the second as the tension built. Brad wasn't sure who was going to explode first. He gave one final glance toward his mother, hoping for once in her life she'd stand up for him or show some kind of empathy, sympathy or even pity. Right now, he'd take what he could get. But she sat motionless, eyes to the ground, hands tightly clasped on her lap.

"What do you want, Dad?" Brad asked. "Speak your mind for a change. What the *fuck* do you want?" His voice sounded so distant, so foreign, he wasn't even sure he was the one speaking.

His father scooted forward in his chair. "First of all, watch your language. Secondly, what do you mean, 'what do you *want?*'" Brad heard a slight tremble of anger in his voice, a minor show of weakness his father had never revealed before. He repeated the question. "What the hell does that mean, 'what do I want?'"

"What do you want? What do you want me to tell you? What do you want to hear? What do you want me to do about this? About everything? What the fuck do you want? You're dancing around the issues like a scared rat trying to scrounge up food, but instead you're trying to scrounge something out of me and I don't have anything to give. I don't know what the hell you want from me!"

As his father's eyes widened, Brad straightened his posture. If the man came after him, he'd have to be prepared to defend himself. And even if his father didn't assault him, he'd most likely have to be ready to walk up the stairs, throw some clothes into a suitcase and walk out.

No matter what happened next, the blood rushing to his head was telling him this wasn't going to end well.

"You ungrateful little shit. After everything, *everything* I've given you, *everything* I've done for you, you have the audacity to go behind our backs to that whore who got knocked up so she could become a Sheehan heir. And if that wasn't bad enough, you've become nothing more than a low-life drug addict who is no better than those dirty, homeless creatures living under the freeway." He covered his face with his hands and then let them slide down onto the arms of the chair, grabbing each one so hard Brad watched his knuckles turn white. "You do this to *me* and ask me what *I* want as though *I've* done something wrong?"

Brad went numb as he rose with the power from some unknown energy. He was on autopilot, the actions he was taking coming from a part of his subconscious over which he had no control.

"You call *me* an ungrateful little shit? *Me?* My entire life you order me around like a soldier. You tell me what to wear, how to act, what school I'll attend, who I can love. You pretty much run every aspect of my life through guilt and coercion, dangling money in front of me like a carrot, bribing me so I'll stay on the path *you* want me to follow. And I walk that path every Goddamn day to keep *you* happy. *You! You're* the ungrateful little shit!"

His father stood up and moved so close, Brad could feel the heat of the man's breath on his face. Brad didn't give him a chance to speak.

"You wonder why I keep things hidden from you? Why I take drugs? Why I live so many lies? It's because I'll never live up to your expectations. No matter what I do, it's wrong. No matter where I study or how much I work out or what friends I have, it's wrong. I can never please you." He felt the warmth of the tears flowing down his cheeks, but he didn't care. His voice was still strong, his body still numb.

"So I had to find something, anything to keep myself from feeling!" He leaned over toward the table with the drugs, grabbed the edge and threw it halfway across the room. The pills scattered everywhere and the table rolled until it hit the wall and stopped moving. He grabbed the phone from his father's hand and headed toward the stairs. "So if you want to blame someone for your loser of a son, take a look in the mirror. When you finally see what I see, we can have a discussion. Until then, I'm out of here."

Feeling like he'd just gotten tackled by a three-hundred-pound lineman, Brad marched up the stairs and walked straight down the hallway to his bedroom. He slammed the door behind him and leaned with his back against it as he tried to catch his breath. When he glanced around the room, it appeared exactly has he imagined: it was in shambles. His father had ransacked every drawer, every closet, every nook and cranny of the room in order to present his display of disgust.

Brad pushed the mattress back onto the bed's box spring and fell on top of it. Exhausted, he curled up and tried to think of another place he might have stashed some drugs. He looked around the ransacked room, eyeing every raided inch, then closed his eyes in an attempt to remember if he'd planned for something like this. Maybe he'd hidden some coke or pills in a location that would be impossible for anyone to find. If he did, he'd also made it impossible for himself to find because he couldn't come up with a thing.

The typical fog, filled with sadness and hopelessness, gripped him again and the more he tried to fight it, the heavier it became. He even yelled at it, screamed "leave me the fuck alone!" but it persisted, clawing at his skull, clutching at his gut. He knew that nothing except for drugs could help him battle what was going on inside of him and now he didn't even have those to help him in the fight.

He surrendered to the emotions flow from deep inside – sobbing like he hadn't since he was five years old. The release felt good but in the back of his mind, somewhere deep in the crevasses of his brain, he knew the emotional relief would in no way make up for the reality of where his outburst was about to lead.

His father would never look in the mirror; never admit to a mistake; never accept a son who not only had a drug problem, but one who didn't have it in him to live up to his impossible expectations. As he tried to catch his breath, he wiped his tears on his blanket and felt a slam to his gut as he realized there were only two outcomes to the situation: he'd have to beg his father for forgiveness, pray that he'd receive it and then suffer through the next two years without pride, dignity or Felicia. Or, he'd need to pack a suitcase, find a job, and somehow make a life for himself and Felicia without any help from his parents.

He thought about Felicia and the expression of both love and sadness she held during their entire time together today. He'd already scarred her by getting her pregnant and now, with what had just happened with his father, he knew he'd have to tell her he was a drug addict. There was no way to hide it anymore. Would she stick with him and help him work through it? Would she still love him? Would she run away and start a new life with someone else?

That's what she should do, he thought. He'd already ruined her life enough. Having to deal with his addictions would only make things worse for her. But he couldn't live without her, nor could he figure out a way to survive on his own without any work experience or contacts who could help. Her career was just starting and the thought of making her give that up so she could work in a shitty retail store to help pay the rent in some rundown apartment in Roxbury or the South End of Boston made him sick to his stomach.

That's when the heavy fog within transformed into an ugly sensation of getting sucked into a black hole that made him feel out of control, his hopelessness spiraling like a vortex of dark thoughts and overwhelming grief.

Until he saw his third option.

Wound up in the corner of the top shelf of his open closet was the workout rope he used at the gym. He used it for his wave and throw exercises to help build his upper body, arms and core. Moving his gaze toward the silhouette of the oak tree right outside his window, he focused on the branch he used to climb as a little boy. He knew, without a doubt, it was still close enough to reach and could easily hold more than two hundred pounds if he decided to use the rope to employ his third option – an alternative that would stop him from further disappointing his father, allow Felicia to find someone who could take care of her like he couldn't, all while freeing himself from the swirling, dark fog that had besieged him most of his life.

He jumped up, grabbed the rope from the closet and threw it onto the bed. Opening the window, he looked out into the darkness of the creek. He thought he heard the sound of laughter – perhaps from someone rafting in the water below. It didn't really matter. Laughter was as foreign to him as all the emotions now passing through his body.

Brad placed the rope on the window ledge. He took the phone from his bed and tapped the message icon that held Felicia's photo.

I'll love you forever, he typed.

He hit "send" and, unable to endure seeing her response, he turned off the phone and stepped carefully out the window and onto the branch.

CHAPTER 13

The scream was so bone-chilling it sent a shock through Mia's entire body. She slammed shut the laptop on which she was searching for the Metro North train schedule and threw it onto the sofa cushion beside her.

"Joel!" she yelled, running from the living room toward the stairs. "Joel! What's going on? Are you okay?"

"Oh my God, Mia! I can't... I don't... Oh God!"

As her mind filled with images of Dave's death only two days before, Mia hurried up the steps, dreading the possibility that she'd have to bear witness to even more horror. Was Joel having a panic attack? Did he cut himself? Would she have to see more blood?

Her heart raced and head spun as she dashed to the third floor. She stood on the landing waiting to hear Joel's voice, but there were a few seconds of silence before she heard a soft groan coming from the study. She turned and ran toward the sound. She found Joel curled up on the floor between the desk and the window, holding a pair of binoculars in one hand and wiping his tears with the other.

She fell on her knees beside him. "Joel! What is it? What happened?"

Still hunched on the floor, Joel pointed up toward the window. He tried to speak through his sniffling while also trying to catch his breath.

Unable to make sense out of his behavior, Mia stood and looked out the large, paned window. Across the creek she could see the blue and white flashing lights of police cars. *Oh my God.* She squinted to see better, but it didn't help. She wasn't even sure if she *wanted* to see what was happening.

The flashing lights were enough to hollow out her stomach and fill it with the sharp, stabbing pain of losing Dave. Scenes of what happened in her bedroom flashed in and out of her mind's eye like a strobe light. Making love with Dave... Tom's voice... the gun in his hand... the gunshot... the blood... the expression on Dave's face. She closed her eyes and shook her head, trying to rattle the images from her head. When she opened her eyes, Joel still sat on the floor, the binoculars hanging from his hand, crying so hard his inhalation was stuttered.

Even though her urge was to run from the study and into her bedroom, she knew she couldn't leave Joel. He was too upset and she worried for his mental welfare – like hers was any more substantial. Even so, he had been there for her, now she had to be there for him.

She peered out the window again but could still only see flashing police lights and something that looked like a searchlight up in the tree.

"That's the Sheehan's house," she said. "Joel, give me the binoculars."

He shook his head. "No, you've been through enough."

She sighed and took in a big breath. "Joel, you make me run up here with a scream that scared me half to death. And now you won't let me see what's going on? Really?"

He grabbed a tissue from the desk and blew his nose. "Yes, really. I shouldn't have screamed like that. I was just... I didn't know..."

She grabbed the binoculars from his hand and ignored Joel as he begged her not to look. She focused the lenses on the scene taking place on the other side of the creek. She gasped and almost fell backward when she saw a body hanging from a tree branch. Two police officers were harnessed to the tree's trunk, apparently positioning themselves to cut the rope and bring the person down to the ground. The officers' movement caused the body to turn and she now saw the boy's face, his eyes still open, staring lifelessly into hers. This time she did fall back, dropping the binoculars onto the hardwood floor.

"Jesus, Joel. That's Brad Sheehan." Her voice trembled.

Joel uttered something unintelligible, his words muffled by his sobs.

Mia leaned her back against the wall beneath the window. She couldn't bear to look outside again.

"Oh my God. Why? Why in God's name would he do something like that?"

Joel shook his head slowly. Without looking up, he grabbed a pill from his pocket and popped it into his mouth.

"It should've been me," he said, struggling to push the tablet down his throat.

Mia winced. "Joel, why would you say that?"

Joel slapped his palm against his birthmark. "*This* is why, Mia! *This!*"

"I don't understand." Mia gently placed her hand on his knee.

"This stain on my face. This thing I've lived with forever that keeps me locked up in the house, without a future, without a life." He covered his eyes with his hands. "And Brad had it all. He was perfect. Smart, sweet, handsome and a future full of promise. *He* should be the one starting his life and I should be the one ending mine."

Mia felt the pain return to her stomach. *Where is this coming from? Did this push him over the edge?* She wondered if being in the house with him for almost three days in a row was making things worse.

"I need to call Martin," she said. As she jumped up to get her phone downstairs, Joel grabbed her hand.

"No!" he said, his voice stronger than it had been since she found him in the room. "He's in a board meeting and said it was one of the most important all year. I'm not going to screw it up for him."

"But I'm worried about you." Mia sat back down next to him on the floor and combed her fingers through his hair. "There's a boy hanging from a tree out there and you're obsessing about your birthmark. Don't you see how strange that is?"

Joel took a deep breath and let it out slowly. "You're right. You're right. I know you're right. I'm sorry. I have a weak mind. Maybe everything that happened even before Brad was too much. And now this. I think I'm losing it." He let his head fall into his open hands.

Mia closed her eyes and took her own deep breath. Had she not been through enough herself? Would she be able to take care of Joel, too? She kept her eyes closed and took another breath. She had no choice, she'd have to keep him as stable as possible until Martin got home. Right now, he was her rock, no matter how many gouges and cracks had started to appear. She felt a jolt of self-pity when it hit her that Joel was pretty much all she had.

She took his hand and held it up against her cheek.

"I get it, Joel. Everything that's gone on over the past few days is a lot to take." She pushed back against her own angst and focused on the man in front of her. "But let's try to deal with everything the best we can. That means breathing, talking things out and not allowing our minds to go to places they shouldn't. Doing that will only make things worse."

He looked up at her and offered a slight smile through his tears.

"You're right," he said. "I know you're right. And I'm sorry. You've been through a lot more than me. I have no right to break down like this."

Mia felt a slight sense of relief, but not enough to make her comfortable about his state of mind. He was speaking more coherently but she wasn't sure if anything she said was sinking in, let alone helping in any way. If there was a landline phone in the study, she'd grab it and call Martin whether Joel wanted her to or not. But both cell phones were downstairs and Joel held her hand so tightly, he clearly wasn't going to let her leave him.

"I bet his father pushed him too hard," he murmured.

"What?" Mia tried to let go of his hand. He held it tighter. "What are you talking about?"

"The man is an obnoxious asshole. Whenever he'd come to a fundraiser or something at the house, he'd talk about Brad. But it was never, 'I'm so proud of my son,' it was always, 'I'm having him do this, so he can become this' or 'I'm making sure he keeps in shape so that his mind stays strong.' He was pushing the poor kid all the time. I swear, I could almost see it in Brad's face when he'd jog past the house. He looked like running was a chore, something he was being forced to do. He probably pushed him beyond his limits and it was too much for Brad to take. Sort of like..."

Joel stopped mid-sentence and looked up at the window.

"Sort of like what?" Mia asked.

"Nothing."

"Sort of like what, Joel?" Her tone was stern, determined to get to the bottom of all his bizarre comments.

"Like the kids who tortured me growing up." More tears fell from his eyes like a faucet had been turned on. "Every day, every Goddamn day. They would torture me about this." He banged his birthmark again with his fist. "It wasn't until tenth grade that I finally convinced my parents to let me get home-schooled. But by that time, the damage had been done and I was a mess. Anxiety turned into panic attacks. Panic attacks into phobias. Phobias into... Well, you can see it for yourself. I can't leave this fucking house. If I was as brave as Brad, I would've hung myself years ago."

Mia's hand was covered with Joel's tears. *Oh shit, he's losing it again. Bring him back. Bring him back.*

"And what about Martin? Does his life mean nothing?"

Joel looked up, tears still sliding over his crimson eyelids. "What do you mean?"

"I mean the man loves you with all his heart. You are his world. Do you think he wants to come home and find you hanging from a tree branch?"

Joel let his head hang down.

"I had my issues too, Joel. I had my problems. And I thought about running away time and time again. But what would that have done to Dave? He would've been devastated. As devastated as I was when..."

Mia felt sick to her stomach as the reality of what had happened to Dave, Tom and her entire life crawled through her veins. She tried to let go of Joel's hand, but he pulled her closer and reached around to hug her.

194

"I'm sorry, Mia. I'm so sorry. I'm crying like a two-year-old about a stupid birthmark while you've been through... God... while you've been through hell. I'm so sorry."

She swallowed hard to hold back the tears. Two of them sobbing like infants wouldn't help anyone. Gently grasping the back of his neck, she pulled him closer and kissed his birthmark.

"Don't apologize, Joel. A lot has happened." She looked upward and out the window. The sky was black, the spotlight gone but the police and ambulance lights continued to flash. There was a dim glow coming from one upstairs window of the house. *What,* she wondered, *are his parents going through right now? Are they somewhere within that beam of yellow incandescence crying and screaming as she was when Dave was killed? Or are they sitting in silence, asking themselves where things went wrong and what signs they might have missed?* "And now this. I just can't believe it. That poor boy. This is just surreal. What is going on?"

Joel leaned back against the wall and combed his fingers through his hair. "Something's not right with this, Mia. All these things happening in such a short period of time. Something is definitely off."

"What are you saying? I don't understand."

Joel wiped his eyes without responding.

"Tell me what you're thinking, Joel. I need to know. Maybe it will help me make some sense out of this madness."

Joel wiped his face dry with the bottom of his tee shirt. "You've been seeing Dave for a year. No one but me knew anything about it. Then all of a sudden, Tom comes home in the middle of the day with a gun in his hand. Why?"

Mia's stomach tightened.

"I don't know," she said, her voice trembling.

"Was he acting any different that day when he left for work?"

"No," she said. "No different. He was actually nicer than usual."

"So Tom comes home and kills poor Dave. Then he shoots *himself* on the shoulder of I-95. Really? Tom? The guy who could sell ice to an Eskimo? Why wouldn't he even *attempt* to use a crime of passion or temporary insanity defense? And now Brad. Three deaths in three days? Doesn't that seem strange to you?"

Mia nodded, unsure if she agreed with him or simply had no other reaction to offer.

"So what are you thinking?" she asked.

"Honestly?"

Mia rolled her eyes. "Of course!"

"I don't want you to think I'm crazy."

"I promise," she placed her hand over her heart. "I won't think you're crazy."

Joel picked at a cuticle, then another before he found the courage to speak. "I think someone's behind this," he said, seemingly embarrassed by his own statement.

Mia edged her head toward his. "What? Where did you come up with that?" She was getting herself ready to break loose, run down the stairs and get the phone to call Martin. Was he talking about himself or someone else? Did Joel somehow make these things happen? She felt a wave of panic race from her stomach to her throat.

"I'm not one hundred percent sure. I just have a feeling. I work from home and I pretty much see everything that goes on around this part of the neighborhood."

"And?" She waited. He didn't respond. "And? What did you see?"

"I don't want to make any false accusations. It's not fair. Especially since I have no evidence to back it up."

She gently shook him. "Spit it out, Joel."

"Scott Atwood," he finally said. As though he knew he had to back up his accusation, Joel let the words flow. "A minute or so before Tom came screeching down the street, I saw Scott cross the street toward your house, then turn around and cross back toward his own house."

Mia stood and leaned her back against the wall. She shook her head in disbelief at Joel's accusation. "So what? Why does Scott crossing the street have anything to do with Dave or Tom or even Brad for that matter? I'm not sure I understand where this is going."

Joel exhaled through tightened lips. "Like I said, I don't want to make false accusations."

"Jesus, Joel. There's a reason you're thinking this. You have to tell me. If I think you're wrong, I'll tell you." Her concern that Joel reached the edge had peaked. She made the decision that if he came out with any more crazy talk, she'd run down the stairs, grab her cell phone and call Martin from outside the house so that Joel couldn't stop her. She held her breath, waiting to hear what he'd come up with next.

"Okay. Okay." Joel slowly stood and walked to the other side of the room, making sure to avoid looking out the window. "I didn't really think about Scott until... well, until Brad. Like I said, his father is a real asshole and if he found out that..."

Joel stopped talking and picked at his birthmark. He looked at Mia.

"If he found out what?"

After a few seconds, Joel continued. "That Brad was a drug addict."

Mia felt another stomach twinge and walked closer to Joel.

"What are you talking about? Brad Sheehan? A drug addict? Why would you think that?"

Joel shamefully pointed to the binoculars.

It took Mia a few seconds before she understood his gesture. "You spied on him?"

Joel nodded, his face turning red.

"Oh my God, Joel." She looked out the window at the Sheehan's house, then quickly turned away. The thought of Joel snooping on Brad made her feel both sick to her stomach and angry. It also made her feel pity for him, so she decided not to berate him and make him feel worse than he probably already did. She also didn't want to risk pulling him off track. If only one piece of Joel's wild theory was correct, it might help her get to the bottom of what had become of her life. "I get it, Joel. I really do. Martin is out a lot on business. You're stuck inside. You need things to stay occupied. I don't agree with what you did. That's a given. But I get it. I really do."

She searched his face, hoping for an indication that he believed her. When he subtly raised the corners of his mouth, she knew she'd seen the sign.

"Thank you," he mumbled.

"Tell me about the drugs," she requested.

"I can't say for sure what drugs they were. Sometimes I'd see him snort something off his window sill or desk. Other times I'd see him taking pills."

Holy shit, Mia thought, *he* really *watched this boy. I can't believe this.*

"And you could see all that from here? How can you be sure they were drugs?"

"Mia, the Sheehans' house is only like seven or eight hundred feet away. Those binoculars can see miles away." He paused. "Plus I know what snorting cocaine and popping pills looks like."

Mia nodded for him to continue. Any more questions might get him so angry or self-conscious he'd stop talking altogether.

"I'm sure when I gave you the binoculars, you didn't look into Brad's room. But I *did*. And it was a mess, like it had been ransacked. Brad wasn't like that. He was anal about neatness, almost OCD. Everything was always in its place. That's why..." He took a breath and ran his fingers through his hair. "That's why, and this all could be my vivid imagination, that's why I have a feeling that someone told his father about the drugs and the man went berserk... searching through his drawers, closets and everything else."

"Jesus, Joel. That's a lot of conjecture." Even though she thought most of what Joel was say *was* his imagination, probably caused by solitude and loneliness, she decided to play along. "Let's, for a minute, say you're right. What does this have to do with Scott Atwood?"

"I told Scott about Brad's drug problem yesterday."

"And?"

"And I knew about the drug issue since I, well, I was watching him. Yes, it was inappropriate, but..." He shrugged, looking down. "There's no one else who would know. No one except for Scott – because I told him."

"And you think Scott told Brad's father?"

Joel thought hard for a moment and then his eyes lit up. "Or he got someone else to do it. Or he tipped him off. Or... I don't know. All I know is that I told him about it yesterday and today Brad is dead."

"But why? Why would Scott do that to Brad?"

Joel grabbed his chin and shook his head in bewilderment. "I have no idea, Mia. Maybe I'm just grasping at straws trying to find a reason for all of this. Forget I even brought it up."

"Oh, okay Joel. I'll just forget you brought it up." Her sarcasm sliced through the thickness of the air between them. She slid her hands into her jeans pockets and paced the floor. "Maybe you're the one who should be writing novels. You have quite an imagination."

"Yeah, well, maybe it's not all imagination, Mia." The annoyance in his voice was palpable. "Remember when he was here yesterday?" She nodded. "Well, before you came downstairs, we were talking. He had already pretty much put the whole thing together – what you and Dave were doing, that Tom came home and caught you. And then it was like he was trying to get more information out of me. I mean, how would he know all of that stuff?"

"I'm sure there were news stories and I'm also sure the police told people they questioned what was going on. Why is it so unrealistic that Scott would know the story, or at least be able to piece it together? Your accusation doesn't make sense. I just can't buy this, Joel."

"Then don't," he whispered.

Mia continued pacing the floor. She considered Joel's suggestion that Scott informed Brad's family about his addiction and threw it out almost as quickly as it appeared. *Preposterous.* Neither she nor Joel even knew if Brad killed himself because his father discovered his addiction. Joel's accusation was all circumstantial evidence, a presumptive fantasy by a man who Mia just discovered spent his nights, and God knows how many days, meddling in other people's business and making up stories in his lonely, twisted mind.

And blaming Scott Atwood? The man who was doing everything in his power to help her get through the toughest time of her life? That was where Joel's story truly went off track. He'd seen two innocuous actions taken by two people he barely knew and had created his own psychological thriller.

She wondered if she should try bringing Joel back to earth by offering realistic explanations. Perhaps it was simply that Brad suffered from depression or was doing poorly in medical school and could no longer stand the pressure. It could've been that Scott was out taking a walk and realized he forgot his keys so he turned around and walked back toward his house. There are too many reasons to count why someone would kill themselves or a person would return to their home in the midst of a walk and Joel was choosing the worst possible scenarios.

She loved Joel; he'd been her closest friend and confidant for almost two years. But she was now questioning his stability and realized she could no longer trust him to help her figure out how to move forward. She started to panic again, worried that she was truly alone and had absolutely no one to count on but herself.

"You know how much Scott is helping me, right Joel?"

Joel nodded.

"With everything he's doing for me, I can't imagine he's behind anything like what you're inferring. He's a writer. A famous author.

He doesn't have time to snoop and spy and get involved in this neighborhood's bullshit. And yet here he is, opening up his heart – and his wallet – to help me get through one of the most difficult times of my life. How can you expect me to think he's the devil in disguise?"

"Mia, I told you it would sound crazy. And I could be totally off base. Everything that's happened could be coincidental. I'm just telling you what I think. You said I should."

"I know. I know I told you to tell me what you're thinking, but it just sounds like you're speculating and making up stories because..."

"Because why?"

Mia felt her emotions start to tear at all ends. She had nothing left and at this point didn't have the energy to hold anything back.

"Because you're alone so much and you have nothing to do but invent tales to keep yourself entertained." She put her hands over her face. "I'm sorry. I just can't deal with everything that's happened. And now you telling me about your spying, and coming up with stories, speculating about Scott. It's just too much for me, Joel. Just too much."

She felt the tickle of a tear roll down her cheek.

Joel was silent. He looked down to the floor and traced the wood grain with the toe of his socked foot.

His voice was soft, trembling as though he was on the verge of crying again. "I told you I didn't want to make any false accusations. But you made me say what I was thinking. So why are you so upset? Are you falling for him or something?"

Mia felt like she'd been punched in the gut.

"*Falling* for him?" She paced the floor, more chaotic thoughts banging around the inside of her head. "Please tell me you're not serious, Joel. I just lost the love of my life... the man I wanted to spend the rest of my life with. And you ask me if I'm falling for Scott Atwood?" It was now *her* voice that was trembling. She couldn't keep it in any longer. "Oh my God, Joel. I really think you've lost your mind."

With that, Mia headed toward the door and ran down the staircase.

"Mia!" Joel yelled, running after her. "Where are you going?"

Mia didn't answer. Not only because she was done talking with him, but she also had no idea where she was headed. All she knew was that she was going to pack her bags and leave. The voice in her head was screaming for her to get away from what she'd witnessed across the creek and everything Joel had just told her.

She grabbed her suitcase from the guest room closet, threw it onto the bed, took the few clothes she had hanging on the rack and tossed them inside the luggage. Hearing Joel's footsteps pattering down the stairs, she rushed to the bathroom to grab her cosmetics and other necessities so she could get them into the suitcase and zip it shut before he made it to the bedroom.

"Mia!" he yelled, stopping at the door. "What did I do? Why are you leaving?"

Mia grabbed the handle of the suitcase and turned to face him. "I don't know where I'm going, Joel. I just know that I need to leave. I think I've overstayed my welcome."

Joel edged closer but stopped when Mia held up her hand.

"Mia, maybe what I said isn't true. Maybe I did make it all up in my head. But let's talk about it. I thought we were good enough friends that we could talk to each other about anything." He paused and looked to the ceiling, his eyes welling up with tears. "Is it because I told you I was watching Brad from the study?"

That's just the start, Mia thought. Sure, she had her own transgressions to work through. She knew she was far from perfect, but the idea that Joel was spying on an innocent boy half his age, and that he now had the audacity to blame Scott for the terrible deaths occurring in the neighborhood, made her sick to her stomach. But she couldn't tell him that. He was too frail, both physically and mentally, and she didn't want to be responsible for any self-harming actions he might take. There'd been enough of those over the past two days. Once she left the house, she'd call Martin, tell him she'd left and urge him to come home.

"No, it's not you watching Brad," she lied.

Unable to look him in the eyes, she walked right past him and into the living room. She grabbed her phone off the table, pocketbook from the sofa and headed toward the front door. "It's everything. It's everything that's happened. It's me feeling guilty that I've invaded your home. It's the fact that I looked out your study window and saw a beautiful young man hanging from a tree." Mia tossed her head back and pushed the lump in her throat as far down as she could. "I just need to get away. To someplace different. It's not your fault, Joel. I swear. It's not."

Joel followed closely behind her until she reached the front door. "I know.... 'It's not you, it's me.' I've heard it so many times, I'm used to it."

Mia walked outside and let the screen door close between them. "Please don't, Joel. I'm already on the edge and right now I have to think about myself... what *I* need. And if you're a real friend, you'll accept that and let me be."

Joel wiped the tears from his cheeks and brushed the hair away from his eyes. "But where are you going to go?"

Again Mia didn't respond. *Away from you,* she thought.

She silently headed down the walkway, across the driveway and made a left onto the sidewalk toward the home of the only person she felt could provide the comfort, help and sanity she needed so badly: Scott Atwood.

CHAPTER 14

Scott pressed the remote button three times to make sure the blinds covering every window overlooking the creek were closed. He didn't want Mia seeing the flashing lights or any other sign of the Sheehans' house; anything to remind the woman sitting on the sofa across from him what she'd seen across the creek just a few hours before.

Although she spoke coherently when she'd first arrived, her monotone timbre and blank expression made him think she was on the edge of an emotional breakdown. He offered her a vodka tonic, which she immediately accepted. After a few minutes of sitting in silence, he leaned forward and clasped his hands.

"So, what exactly..." he started.

"I'd rather not talk about Joel," Mia interrupted. "I just can't right now."

"I get it," Scott replied, slowly reclining back against the chair.

"This whole thing is crazy, Scott. First Dave, then Tom, now Brad. One murder and two suicides. All in the matter of three days. And Jesus, one was my husband and..." her voice started to tremble, "and one was the love of my life." She closed her eyes and the look on her face made Scott think she might pass out. When she opened them, he let out a sigh of relief. "It's like I'm living in an alternate reality. Like someone is playing a sick joke on me and if I find the secret key, I'll wake up and everything will be normal again."

Scott wasn't sure what she meant by "secret key" or where her thoughts were leading her, but he let her continue. He feared stopping her vent might make her think he wasn't willing to listen. But he was. He was ready to do anything she wanted him to do.

She took another sip of her drink and wiped the tears from her cheeks. "If all of this wasn't happening in real life, I'd think I was reading one of your books."

Scott felt a jolt of electricity roll through him. *If you only knew.* And then the memory of his conversation with Jordan ripped into his head, those few words he subtly slipped in about Brad's drug problem. *Could that have anything to do with what happened tonight? Did I cause someone else to die? Am I now a triple murderer? Have I become...*

"Scott? Did you hear me?" Mia was now yelling.

Scott shook his head, trying to gain some clarity. "What? No. I'm sorry. What did you say?"

"I asked you what was wrong. You grabbed your arm as though you were in pain. And by the look on your face, you *are* in pain. What's going on?"

Shit. This goddamn arm.

"Nothing, Mia. It's nothing. I'm fine. I think it's a nerve issue. I'm getting it checked out next week."

"Can I get you something? Aspirin? Ibuprofen?"

Scott feigned a laugh. "It plays with me. It'll go away in a few minutes. I just have to relax it a little."

"It's not funny. It could be the sign of something more..."

"Don't, Mia. This isn't about me. We need to figure out what the hell is going on. All of these events happening like this isn't possible – *even in a fictional book.*"

He sounded so serious about getting to the truth, he almost convinced himself that he wasn't responsible. Sure, he deserved everything he was feeling, from the agonizing shame in his gut to the excruciating ache in his arm. But tough shit on him. He had a week left to get the book to Grace and nothing was going to stop him.

"I think we already know most of the 'whys.'" She swirled the vodka around her mouth, then gently swallowed. Scott watched carefully, captivated by her every move. "I mean, we know why Tom killed Dave. He was probably devastated and wanted to take away any happiness I could find with someone else." She shook her head, the pain and disbelief still evident in the shape of her eyes. "I sometimes wonder why he didn't kill me, too. And then I remember who Tom was and realize he'd rather me live and suffer than have me die and be at peace. Tom was a coward. He always had been. That's why he killed Dave and that's why he killed himself. He couldn't ever deal with reality. Ever." She took a deep breath. "I just don't understand why Brad would do this to himself. Jesus, Scott, this neighborhood has become a breeding ground of death and chaos. Honestly, I haven't even had the time to process what happened to Dave. I know he's gone, I know Tom killed him, but it just doesn't seem real. Nothing seems real anymore." She turned her head away from where the flashing lights continued to creep through the blinds. "I think you're right about me getting away from here. At least for the day. I need to clear my head in another space."

As the pain in Scott's arm lessened, the excitement in his chest grew. Mia was taking him up on his offer to get away with him, and this glimmer of hope made him smile. Yeah, she definitely had a lot of shit to work through, but he would be there every step of the way. Whatever Mia wanted, Mia would get. He closed his eyes for a few seconds, hoping he'd be one of the things she'd want... and soon.

"I think we both need to clear our heads," Scott said, almost whispering.

"How's your arm? You sound like you're still in pain."

He rubbed his arm and rested his hand on his shoulder. "It's sort of eased up a bit. Like I said, I'll be getting it checked next week."

A few moments of silence passed before Scott rested his arm along the back of the sofa. He picked at the frayed linen, unsure what he should say next. *Screw it.*

"Okay, I want you to stay here tonight." Mia stared directly into his eyes, a look of fear and distrust seizing her face. "You can stay in the study on the fold-out couch or in one of the bedrooms down here. It's completely up to you. I'll be in my room upstairs." To his relief, the panic in her expression waned. "I'll call Larry now and tell him we'll meet him at the Park Avenue office tomorrow. I'll make sure he brings in lunch."

"So you can just call your lawyer whenever you want and he'll meet you at the drop of a hat? Even on a Sunday?"

Scott smirked. "With the money he's made off my career, I've pretty much bought his house in the Hamptons and paid for his daughter's MIT education. He'll meet us when and where we want."

"Okay. But honestly, if everything goes through for me, like a decent inheritance, pension or whatever, I want to pay you back. Tom never discussed finances with me, so I have no idea if he left me anything or not. I just know I *need* to pay you back because it will make me feel better."

"Got it. I understand. We'll discuss it when the time comes," he said, slightly disappointed. Sleeping with him was the only way he wanted her to pay him back but he knew that would take some more time. *Can you show some compassion? Jesus Christ!* "And while we're on our way to the city, I'll call Detective Jordan to see if he knows anything about the Sheehan situation. Maybe he can tell us something that can make us both feel a little better about what's going on." *Just shut up, you lying sack of shit. You know it's your fault.* "Maybe he can shed some light on what happened and why. Something that can confirm the fact that there's not a maniac running loose making people do crazy things."

"Detective Jordan is a very nice man," Mia said. "The night Dave... the night Tom shot..." Tears started to fill her eyes again.

"It's okay," Scott said soothingly. "I know it's still raw for you."

Mia nodded and cleared her throat. "Detective Jordan seemed like a compassionate person. Like he wants to get the job done right but also cares about the people he's dealing with. He snuck me out of my house, past the nosy neighbors and the press, and got me to Joel's."

"I know," Scott said. "You told me that Thursday."

"Geez. That's right. Two days feels like two months." She pulled her hair back behind her ears. "How well do you know Detective Jordan?"

"He's helped me with a few of my books. You know, making sure I have the police procedural part of my stories correct. I pay him back with good dinners and lots of Johnnie Walker Blue."

Mia picked up her glass and took another sip. "Has he told you anything about me? You know, about Dave or Tom or anything that might be happening with the case?"

"Absolutely not." Scott stood and walked to the bar. Right now, he was the one in need of some Johnnie Walker Blue. "He never shares information like that."

Mia nodded slowly. "So then why would he give you information about Brad?"

Oh shit. Good question.

Scott took a slug of scotch and let himself enjoy the slow burn as it trickled down his throat. He was getting tangled up in his web of lies, and every time he opened his mouth he found it more difficult to unravel himself.

"I don't know. Maybe he'll slip up and give something away. Maybe... I... I'm not sure, really. I just want to find out what's going on and have to take any chance I can. I guess I'm desperate to answer these questions and bring a little normalcy back to this town."

Except for a yawn she attempted to disguise, Mia had no reaction. Her drowsiness was the perfect excuse for him to escape the conversation and separate for the night before he said anything else that could get him into trouble. He stood, walked into the kitchen and placed his glass in the sink. When he returned the living room, Mia was standing, suitcase in one hand and pocketbook in the other. Her confused expression told Scott he'd be the one making the decision about where she'd sleep.

"Why don't you take the room down the hall? It has its own bathroom with clean towels and clean linens on the bed. Just make yourself at home. I'll be upstairs if you need anything." She didn't move. "By the way, I think there's a 10:10 train to Manhattan tomorrow. Is that okay with you or did you want to sleep in?"

"I'll probably be up way before then. I haven't slept much lately. 10:10 is fine."

Scott slid his hands into his pant pockets and shifted from side to side. He wasn't sure how to end the night and hoped his uneasiness was less evident to Mia than it was to himself.

"Like I said, if you need anything I'll be right upstairs. And don't worry, the door has a lock on it just in case you don't trust me." *Idiot! Why would you say that?*

"Stop that! Of *course* I trust you." Mia walked around the edge of the sofa and started to make her way down the hallway. She stopped suddenly and turned around. "Right now, Scott, you're the only person I trust. Goodnight."

"Goodnight," he responded as she entered the room and closed the door. He waited for a full minute, listening to see if she'd lock the door. There was nothing but silence.

She really does *trust me.*

Walking up the stairs to his bedroom, he stopped on the landing and gazed out the giant bay window. There were no more flashing lights, no more police cars, no more rope hanging from a tree. The horror from the day had been cleaned up as though it had never happened.

But it did. And the pain in Scott's arm was a sign to him that one way or the other, by either his own actions or those of another, he was going to pay for it.

***

Mia turned over and over in bed, unable to get comfortable or keep her eyes closed for more than a few seconds. She puffed the pillow, straightened the blanket, even tried counting backward from one thousand. Nothing was working. She looked over at the neon blue digits staring at her from the clock sitting on the nightstand: 2:11 AM.

Shit. Three hours of tossing and turning. I'm going to be a mess tomorrow.

The queen size bed was more than big enough. The mattress even had memory foam which contoured to every curve of her body. There wasn't a sound coming from anywhere in the house – just the kind of silence anyone would need to fall asleep.

And yet it wasn't happening. Why were the last three hours spent staring at the ceiling, the clock, the amorphous shadows dancing amidst the darkness? Was it the new surroundings? The guilt she felt about leaving Joel and ignoring his calls and texts? Was it the intruding memory of Dave falling backward against the wall from the gunshot? Maybe it was Tom's blank expression as he pulled the trigger. Right now it didn't really make a difference. The fact of the matter was her thoughts starting to overwhelm her and she couldn't help but feel she was about to jump out of her skin.

She thrust her legs over the side of the bed and placed her feet on the wood floor. It was cold. As a matter of fact, she realized she was almost shivering as she stood in her tank top and panties. She searched the dark room for Dave's shirt and spotted where she'd hung it over the arm of the loveseat by the window.

She whispered aloud, "He must have the air conditioning set to sixty degrees."

Making sure not to bang her toes against any furniture, she made her way to the loveseat, grabbed Dave's shirt and slid her arms into the sleeves. She closed her eyes and hugged herself, letting the shirt wrap around her, imagining it was Dave's arms holding her tightly and sharing his warmth with her. She smiled faintly until she opened her eyes and was hit by a darkness and loneliness so heavy she almost lost her breath.

Her anxiety turned into panic and she suddenly felt trapped. As she ran to the door to escape, she heard a soft moan. Terrified, she forced herself to turn around. It wasn't until she heard the sound again that she realized it was coming from somewhere deep within her throat, a place where her grief and anguish had found a home, a place she knew she'd have to fight to reclaim. For now, though, she couldn't find the strength. The battle was just too hard. So she buttoned Dave's shirt, which hung so low its hem almost reached her knees, opened the door and slowly strolled down the long, shadowy hallway toward the center of the giant house.

The bright beam of the full moon lit up the living room. Mia approached the patio windows and looked over the creek at the Sheehan's house. She put her palm up against the glass of the sliding door as though her hand could in some way soothe the soul of the young man who, just hours before, cut his own life short for reasons only he could understand.

Her heart hurt – for Brad, for herself, for every person in the world suffering at that very moment. She took a deep breath and turned around. Straight ahead, on the other side of the house, the streetlamp outside illuminated Scott's office. From where she stood, Mia could see the reflection of light bouncing off the closed cover of his laptop. Suddenly she felt colder, almost frozen, frightened at the sudden temptation to sneak a peek at his newest work. Would reading his new book be as bad as Joel snooping on Brad? No, it was totally different, she thought. *Right? Totally different.* She'd be getting a glimpse into the mind of a creative genius and be able to read a bestselling novel before ink ever hit paper. It wasn't as though she was spying on someone's private life or personal actions. *Right?*

Her lips moved in silence to the shouting in her mind. *Should I? Is it wrong? I'll never tell anyone. No one will ever know.*

With each thought, she took a step closer to Scott's office. When she finally reached the doorway, she glanced back into the living room. The moonlight hid behind the giant elms, creating lengthy shadows across the floor and up onto the walls, a natural work of art that would soon change as the night turned into day.

Other than the sound of her own breathing, Mia didn't hear a thing. There was no doubt Scott was still asleep, and there was also a zero percent chance she'd be able to sleep knowing that she'd missed the opportunity to read a Scott Atwood book before it was even edited.

She ran to the desk and sat in Scott's chair, wrapping Dave's shirt even more tightly around her torso.

"We'll do this together," Mia whispered to Dave.

She felt him in the room, sitting beside her, just as curious to read every word that she was about to devour.

***

Mia shook uncontrollably.

It wasn't the cold air or lack of clothing that made her tremble. And it wasn't the fact that she was reading something she didn't have permission to read. It was the words flying off the screen in front of her, each one like a hammer against her skull, a lashing of her soul that almost left her breathless.

She used Dave's shirt sleeves to wipe the tears running down her face, but found it impossible to hold back a gasp when she read the words that took the insanity of Joel's suspicions and placed them in a whole new light...

If Tom somehow found out about Mia's infidelity, all hell would break loose. Mayhem would ensue and although Mia and Tom's life would disintegrate, Scott's book would start to take shape. This was the perfect conflict to start establishing a plot, and Scott's stomach trembled with excitement. The question was: how could he get Tom to find out about the liaison? It had been going on for about a year and the putz still didn't know.

"Oh my God," she whispered. "What in God's name...?"

This isn't possible, she thought. She rubbed her leg, gently touched her face. Her skin felt warm and solid against her fingers, but she couldn't believe it. She must be dreaming. She read the words again, trying to figure out if she was seeing them correctly or if her eyes, and mind, were playing tricks on her.

Scott wouldn't. No. He couldn't. Not Scott. No.

She continued reading...

In disbelief he watched the Lexus grind to a halt in front of Mia's house, the skidding tires creating a smoke screen behind the car. Scott gasped when Tom opened the door and exited the car with a gun in his hand. He wanted to run outside and up the block. He wanted to stop Tom in his tracks, somehow tell him it was all a big mistake. But then he'd give himself away. He walked away from the window and paced the floor. Holy shit! What should I do? What the hell do I do now? *Scott returned to the window and glanced out the blinds. Tom had disappeared behind the hydrangeas as he headed toward the front door. Scott shook his head in disbelief. It was too late to do anything now but pray.*

Mia could barely see the screen through her tears. She rubbed her arms, trying to stop shivering. She didn't want to read anymore. There had to be a mistake. This wasn't the Scott she knew, the Scott she trusted. This was a monster who apparently used her life to create a work of fiction. She jumped up and was about to close the laptop and run into the room to grab her bags when she took one last look at the screen...

In a few hours he'd discover what Tom had done to Mia and her boyfriend, what devastation and grief he'd caused to save his career, and what kind of guilt he'd have to live with for the rest of his life.

In the meantime, he pushed his face into the sofa and sobbed until he finally lost consciousness.

It was at that point that anger began to warm her veins and the trembling stopped. She sat back down in Scott's chair, wiped the tears from her eyes and leaned forward to make sure she could see every word. There was no turning back now.

CHAPTER 15

Mia sat on the deck that overlooked the creek and held her coffee cup with both hands.

The sun was rising, its shadow of dawn creeping over the Sheehans' house like the hand of death searching for another soul to grab. She turned away and looked in the other direction. From where she sat, she could almost see the edges of Joel's backyard. Pangs of guilt began to erupt, and she tried to push them aside. Even though Joel's insane suspicions about Scott had turned out to be true and she knew he was due an apology, there were more important things to take care of right now.

After reading Scott's book and what he'd written so far, her sadness was now accompanied by rage toward the man she thought was her sole friend and confidant. She had narrowed her options down to three: confront Scott about his book and see how things unfolded; take Scott's laptop to the police and let them handle the situation; get her deserved revenge on the person who had destroyed her life and taken away her one chance at happiness.

Taking another sip of coffee, she looked at her watch: 6:58. She'd already dressed for the day, still uncertain if she'd be going with Scott to Manhattan or staring him down at the police station. The bright red silk tee-shirt she threw on was one of Dave's favorites. He'd say its reflection brought out the blue in her eyes and made him feel like he was swimming in a "pool of Mia." She knew if she were going to have any of her plans come to fruition, she'd need Scott to focus on her so she wore her cutoff denim shorts that reached mid-thigh – long enough to exhibit a speck of modesty but short enough to hold his attention. Since she had only two pairs of footwear with her, she chose the wedge sandals that would help keep her cool on what her weather app told her was going to be one of the hottest days of the summer.

Mia traced the coffee cup rim with her index finger.

"Make a decision," she whispered to herself. *What will it be? Confrontation? Police? Revenge? Confrontation? Police? Revenge? Confrontation? Pol...?*

"Good morning, Mia." Scott's voice came from behind her, through the screened patio door. The surprise of it almost sent her leaping from her chair. "Oh God, I'm sorry if I scared you."

Mia turned around. "It's okay," she lied. Just looking at him made her stomach turn. To think that yesterday she thought of him as her only savior, and today he was her most despised enemy.

He wore a white linen shirt that was so wrinkled she could see the creases through the dark porch screen. His salmon-colored shorts fell slightly above his knees, his legs a shade of pale she'd never quite seen before on any human being. As she worked her gaze down his legs, she offered a quick prayer that if he was wearing sandals he would at least have the common sense not to be wearing socks. Though her prayer was answered, the sight of his feet squished into dark brown Birkenstocks forced her to close her eyes.

This was the Scott Atwood adored by millions? His fans must've only seen him on the back cover of his books or primped and made up for a TV interview, because to see him as she saw him right now would make them think twice about reading another one of his stories. Why didn't she see him like this yesterday? Was she blinded by his generosity? Or was it the fact that just a few hours ago she had discovered this was the man responsible for Dave's death?

She caught herself glaring at him and forced herself to fake a subtle smile.

"There's more coffee in the pot," she said.

"Great," he replied, turning around to walk toward the kitchen. "I'll be back in a sec."

Take your time. Please. Take your time.

Mia took another sip of coffee. She thought she'd have a while longer to make a decision, but with Scott's sudden and early appearance, she knew she was running out of time. If she confronted him, he'd probably accuse her of snooping around and come up with some bullshit story around how what had happened over the past few days only helped *influence* the book's plot. She could almost hear him uttering the words, "I turned non-fiction into fiction. That's all. You're making something out of nothing, Mia." But she knew the truth. By the way he'd written the story and the time stamps on the revisions, she knew whatever he'd say would be a complete lie. Every word in his book was proof that before the disaster which had torn apart her life, Scott had had no story.

If she got the police involved, how could they prove he'd been the root of all the evil that's gone on? Would his detective friend protect him and vouch for his innocence before even looking into the case? And in the end, was anything he'd done illegal? Going to the police would also bring her into the spotlight – again, after the nightmare circus of Dave's murder and Tom's death – and unless she could be one hundred percent sure he'd end up in prison, she didn't want to take that chance.

She thought about calling Joel, begging for forgiveness and asking him for advice. But there was no way she could do that. Not only had she so blatantly blown off his concerns the night before, she'd pretty much called him crazy and ran out on him as he yelled for her to come back. If she were him, she wouldn't answer her calls either.

Revenge. The word rang through her head like the massive echo of a church bell. It sent a vibration from the base of her neck to the soles of her feet. Mia knew this was the only way to handle the situation. Scott Atwood was a madman, a narcissistic psychopath who had no problem destroying other people's lives in order to hold onto his career. The trick now was to hide what she knew from him while at the same time working out how she'd get her revenge.

She started to feel guilty and hadn't even taken any action. This wasn't who she was, it wasn't who she wanted to become. But reading Scott's book as the memory of Dave trying to speak to her as he took his last breath had somehow changed her. It was as though she didn't care... about Scott, herself or life.

"Wow, that's good," Scott said, sliding open the screen door. "You sure know how to make good coffee."

He sat down and placed his cup down on the glass table between them.

Unable to look at him, she gazed out over the creek. She forced herself to catch a glimpse of the Sheehans' house. There were no cars, no movement, nothing. The property looked just as it did yesterday morning at the exact same time. The only difference was that Brad, and the branch from which he hung, were no longer a part of that home.

Although it was almost seventy-five degrees outside and the humidity oppressive, Mia felt a chill through her slight perspiration. She remembered the part of Scott's book in which he told Detective Jordan that Brad would jog past her house. She was positive that was a planting of the seed of suspicion that somehow led to the boy's suicide. Joel was right. This was all just too coincidental. Dave, Tom, Brad. Who was next? Who else would die by this demonic scheme? And how did this maniac plan on ending his book?

"Mia, did you hear me?"

Another chill.

"No, I'm sorry. Just thinking."

"I said you really know how to make great coffee."

She rolled her eyes and then made herself look at Scott.

"Oh, stop." She feigned modesty. It was not, of course, all that she was feigning. "The coffee maker did all the work."

Scott lifted his cup and took another sip. "Yeah, well, tell the coffee maker to work this well for me, because when I make it, it doesn't taste like this." He paused. "And, by the way, that bright red looks great on you."

Mia faked another smile and sipped some more coffee. She was almost unable to swallow it, the acid in her gut creeping up into her throat. Still unable to look at Scott for too long, she glanced up the right side of the creek as though she were watching something of interest. There was nothing but crystal clear water barely making its way over the rocks.

She took in a big breath and let it out slowly, hoping she'd be able get through the day beside this rotten, disgusting piece of —

"I spoke with Hindman before coming downstairs," Scott said.

"Uh-huh."

"He's expecting us around noonish. He wants to take us to one of his favorite brunch places on Park Avenue."

Oh my God, Mia thought. *Why am I doing this? I can't go. I can't. I have to get out of this.*

"I don't know, Scott. I really didn't plan on going to New York to have a fancy brunch and drink mimosas. I thought we were just going to get away for an hour or two and talk through some legal issues with him. Maybe I'm not ready. Maybe I shouldn't go."

Scott took off his glasses and placed them on the table, along with his coffee cup. He stood, took a few steps toward Mia and knelt down in front of her. When he touched her hands, she fought hard not to retch.

"We don't have to do anything you don't want to do, Mia. If you don't want brunch, we won't do brunch. But I do think it's important to get you away from here for a few hours and also get Larry to start the process of taking care of your legal affairs."

She looked into his eyes and restrained herself from spitting in his face by pretending she was talking with a stranger. *Revenge. Revenge. Revenge.* There it was again, echoing over and over inside her head. Mia knew that getting closer to Scott would allow her to retaliate and avenge the death of Dave, along with Brad and even Tom. And since he hadn't yet finished the book, she also had no idea what the next page would reveal. Whose death would he cause next? Who's life was he going to destroy for the sake of keeping his fame and fortune alive? Or was he doing these things just to keep himself occupied because he was such a lonesome, sad, angry man? Her mind was spinning but she had no time to calm it down. Scott was awaiting her answer.

"Okay, we'll go. I'm just not sure about brunch yet." She gently pulled her hands from his. "Let's see how the train ride goes and we'll take it from there. Okay?"

Scott stood and walked back to his chair. "For sure." He took another sip of coffee. "Since you made this coffee, let me make you some breakfast. Will a toasted bagel work? That's about the extent of my cooking repertoire."

Asshole.

"Yes, that will be just fine. Thank you so much."

Scott stood and took a huge stretch as he looked at the creek. "My pleasure. Just give me a few minutes."

Mia didn't say a word as he slid open the screen door and walked inside. She heard his sandaled feet flopping on the rug and getting louder when they hit the kitchen floor. She ran her fingers through her hair and took a deep breath. There was only one thing that was going to get her through this day.

Revenge.

***

As they walked the platform toward the spot where the last few compartments of the train would stop, Scott handed Mia her ticket. He looked at his watch.

"10:08," he said. "We made it with two minutes to spare."

Mia slid the ticket into the back pocket of her shorts and tried to keep up with Scott's rapid steps. It was so hot her sunglasses kept sliding down her nose in sweat. It was only ten o'clock in the morning and it must've already been eighty degrees. She slid her sunglasses up and picked up her pace even more. Why was he walking so fast?

Was he angry? Did he blame her for having only two minutes to spare? Yeah, she did hold them up a bit, but *screw him,* she thought, *he killed my Dave!*

"I'm sorry I took so long," Mia replied. "I'm in a weird state right now. I couldn't even get my eyeliner on straight. My mind isn't working and neither are my hands, I guess."

Scott stopped walking and turned to her. "You look beautiful," he said.

If she didn't hate him so much, she would've given him a peck on the cheek. And by the expression on his face it appeared as if he was expecting one. He continued to walk and she stepped in stride beside him, catching sight of all the other people on their way to Grand Central Station. Some tried to hide from the sun under the narrow overhang of the platform's roof, while others basked under the August sky as though the oppressive heat was somehow invigorating. As they both slowed down, she felt a bead of sweat slowly drip down her back.

This was definitely a mistake. The narrow blocks, crammed buildings and skyscraper-filled streets made New York City at *least* ten degrees hotter than Scarsdale. If she was perspiring now, what would happen when she got off the train at Grand Central? She turned to Scott who leaned over the edge of the platform to look for the arriving train. It didn't appear as though the heat was bothering him.

His cold blood is probably keeping him cool.

He looked down at his watch again. "I don't see it yet. Should be here any minute, though."

Mia didn't respond. The sun beating down on her head was making her a bit woozy. It wasn't so much the dizziness that was affecting her as much as the thoughts stirring around inside her head. Images of Dave walking into the house with his adoring smile, his eyes staring into hers as they lay in bed talking about their future together. The images were stronger and clearer than they'd been over the past few days, and they invoked a rage she hadn't felt since this whole tragedy unfolded. She looked at Scott, whose gaze stretched down the tracks. He smiled and mumbled something she couldn't quite make out, her mind so full her senses were numb. As the visions of all she'd lost grew stronger, so did her rage. The man who had caused all of her pain was standing directly in front of her and the realization that she couldn't suppress her fury any longer seized her entire body.

The rumbling from afar grew louder, the train's approach adding to Mia's anxiety. Her heart pounded and her legs felt paralyzed, but she knew she had to move in order to do what had to be done. As the rumbling got louder, she grabbed Scott's arm.

"I read your book last night," she said.

Scott held his hand to his ear, signaling he couldn't hear her.

"I read your book last night!" she yelled.

He slid off his sunglasses and tried to find her eyes through her dark lenses.

"Which book?" he yelled back.

"The one on your laptop! The one that proves how you were the one who made Tom kill Dave! The one that tells how you helped Brad take his own life!"

As the color rushed from Scott's face, he opened his mouth to respond but no words escaped. Before he had a chance to think it through, Mia tightened her grip on his arm. She turned to look for the train. It was only a few yards away.

"And here's the next chapter... you crazy shit!"

With those words, she pushed him over the side of the platform and closed her eyes as the train carried him away. She fell to her knees and let go of a scream that could have woken the dead. And it should have because then Dave would be holding her, comforting her as the tears rolled down her cheeks. Even Tom would be there to ask what brought on such anguish and pain. But her cry was silenced only by the endless screeching of a passenger train's brakes.

EPILOGUE

Scott felt the cupped hands holding his head from behind. Every few seconds, there was a sense of thin fingers delicately rubbing the base of his skull.

He groaned, his eyelids too heavy to open.

From somewhere in the distance he heard a voice.

"I think he's regaining consciousness," it said.

It wasn't until the words made sense to him that the pain started to radiate throughout his entire body. Almost as bad was the suffocating and intense heat beating down on his face.

"Can someone shield his face from the sun, please?" another voice asked. He could barely make out the words over the screams coming from every side of him.

A few seconds later, the brilliant light that had almost burned through his eyelids turned a silverish gray and the blistering heat vanished. He used all the energy he could summon to open his eyes.

"Hi," a female voice said. It was the woman holding his head in her hands.

When her face finally came into focus, he felt his heart skip a beat.

"Mia," he whispered.

The woman smiled. "No, I'm Sarah and we need you to keep still."

Scott blinked a few times and looked directly into the woman's blue eyes. He moved his gaze down her neck to the bright red silk tee-shirt Mia had on that morning.

"Mia, why? Why would you..."

"Shhh... my name is Sarah." She looked up from Scott to someone directly across from her. "I'm a vet technician helping this Harvard med student save your life. Please help us and relax."

The confusion enveloped Scott like windswept rain. This was the woman who pushed him into an oncoming train and she was acting like a stranger, pretending to help save his life. He closed his eyes and mustered enough strength to lift his head and see the "student" she was referring to.

"Holy shit!" Scott muttered, his throat so dry the words were barely audible. "Brad? Brad Sheehan? How the hell...?"

"Sir," the young man said, wrapping Scott's left foot tightly in a white towel that was rapidly turning red with blood. "My name is Phillip Thomas. I'm not a doctor, but I'm currently attending Harvard Med. To be honest — you're in dire shape. I need you to lay your head down and not expend any energy whatsoever."

"But she tried to kill me!" Scott tried to yell, but only fragments of words escaped his lips. He let his head fall into the hands below him, hearing what sounded like an approaching fire truck or police sirens.

"Kill you?" The voice came from his right side. He slowly turned his head to see another young man kneeling beside him, a birthmark the shape of Italy creeping out from under his knit beanie. "You kiddin' me, dude? She tried to save you from killing yourself." The man looked down to the ground beside Scott and winced. "Guess she couldn't pull you back fast enough."

"Joel," Scott started. The dryness of his throat caused pain in his larynx that felt like a thousand razor blades inching their way down his neck. "What are you talking about? Mia tried to kill me. Didn't you see her push me into the..." Scott stopped mid-sentence, following the man's gaze to see what was making him cringe. Lying beside him, on what looked like a baby's blanket, was a severed arm. When he tried lifting his own arm to grab Joel's leg, he saw nothing but a stump and bloody tourniquet.

He screamed in silence as the pain in his arm ripped through him like a buzzsaw.

"We're trying to get some ice for that," Brad's lookalike said, his tone desperate but professional. "I'm not sure it can be saved, but we have more important things to deal with right now, like getting your vitals under control."

Joel moved sideways to avoid the blood flowing from the detached arm toward his new Nikes. "First of all, who the hell is Joel? My name is Matt. And you're Scott Atwood, aren't you? Read all your books. Would know your mug anywhere."

Scott closed his eyes, unable to move his one remaining arm. He wanted to lay it on his chest and calm the bass drum pounding within his sternum.

What the fuck is going on? Why are these people acting like this... like I'm someone they've never met? Am I dead? Is this hell? Did I go to hell for what I did? Jesus Christ, what have I done?

"Leave the guy alone." A black man, with armpit stains the size of Minnesota soiling his dark blue denim shirt, crossed his arms over his chest. "The guy's half dead," he continued. "What? Ya gonna ask for his autograph next?"

Darryl! Scott yelled in his head, too weak to speak. *Darryl, it's me! You know me. Don't you know me?*

The man grabbed the yellow and blue-striped tie he'd thrown over his shoulder and placed it flatly against his protruding stomach. "Show some respect," he said to the guy calling himself Matt. "Or I'm gonna erase that mark right off your head."

"He doesn't look so good," Matt said, ignoring the man's threat.

And that's when reality came crashing against Scott from all sides.

He recognized the black man with the tie from earlier, when he came to the train station alone to write his book. The same with Phillip. The kid who was now wrapping his foot in a towel had been standing with friends, a hidden logo on his shirt and a sad expression on his face. And Matt, he remembered him too, sitting on the edge of the bench, knees up to his chin. Yeah, these people were all on the platform just before he made the decision to —

Oh God.

That's the moment he saw the beautiful blonde woman in the bright red tee shirt running toward him. She had grabbed his arm to pull him toward her, but the train was already too close. He felt the impact of the train, everything went black and —

Wait. Then who's Mia? Darryl? Joel? What about the three men I was responsible for killing? Dave, Tom and Brad? Where did they come from? Where did they go? Did I lose my mind?

"Scott," Sarah whispered as she brushed the hair off his forehead. "Please take it easy. You can't keep stirring around like that. You need to keep still."

Scott didn't even realize he'd been moving. He was too busy trying to figure out what the hell was going on.

"I can't." He thrashed about. His voice was hoarse, his throat hot as fire. "I have to find Mia and Joel. I have to apologize to the Sheehans. Darryl, I need to speak to Darryl. Where's Darryl?"

Matt pulled his beanie further down over his birthmark. "The guy's losing it." He glanced at Philip, now gently placing Scott's toweled foot onto the concrete platform. "Hey doc, you got any meds for this guy? He's losing it. Either that or he's writin' some crazy, shitass book in his head." Matt laughed at what he thought was a joke.

And then, in a fragment of an instant, Scott made sense of it all.

Mia, Joel, Darryl, all of them. The people surrounding him at this very moment were the characters he'd been creating in his mind while dying on a train platform. The incessant screams he kept hearing... the sirens... the inexplicable arm pain. All part of a crazy man's plot, a man who threw himself in front of a train, convinced his creative well had run dry.

I thought I had nothing left, he cried out to himself. *But holy shit, my imagination had never stopped working. It was always there for me and I want to use it! I want to write this book! God, let me finish this story. Please let me finish this story.*

A tear crawled out the side of his eye.

"It's going to be okay, Scott," the woman holding his head whispered in his ear. "It's going to be okay."

But it wasn't. He could feel the numbness embracing his body, the pain fading away and the voices around him becoming muted and muffled. Closing his eyes, Scott surrendered to the whisper of death that enshrouded him. It wasn't so much because he'd given up on life or that he didn't have any fight left within him.

It was because he knew this would be the perfect ending to the book he had not yet finished... or for that matter, even started.

A Word From Rob

I hope you enjoyed reading "The Perfect Ending" as much as I enjoyed writing it! I'd love to hear your thoughts about the book, the characters and anything else you liked (or didn't)!

You can always write an Amazon review or contact me anytime at Rob@RobKaufmanBooks.com

Also, if you liked "The Perfect Ending", I'm sure you'll enjoy reading my other books. Learn more about them at Amazon…

ONE LAST LIE
A BROKEN REALITY
IN THE SHADOW OF STONE

JUSTIN WRIGHT SUSPENSE SERIES
BOOK 1 – ALTERED
BOOK 2 – JADED
BOOK 3 – AVENGED (coming in June of 2023)

Thanks again for reading "The Perfect Ending"!

To receive emails about my new books, events and news, sign up for my mailing list at www.RobKaufmanBooks.com.